Charles Carroll Everett

Poetry, Comedy, and Duty

Charles Carroll Everett

Poetry, Comedy, and Duty

ISBN/EAN: 9783744768238

Printed in Europe, USA, Canada, Australia, Japan

Cover: Foto ©Andreas Hilbeck / pixelio.de

More available books at **www.hansebooks.com**

POETRY, COMEDY, AND DUTY

BY

C. C. EVERETT, D. D.

BUSSEY PROFESSOR OF THEOLOGY IN HARVARD UNIVERSITY

BOSTON AND NEW YORK
HOUGHTON, MIFFLIN AND COMPANY
The Riverside Press, Cambridge
1896

The Riverside Press, Cambridge, Mass., U. S. A.
Electrotyped and Printed by H. O. Houghton & Company.

PREFACE.

In this volume poetry, comedy, and duty are first considered separately. In the "Conclusion" their relation to one another is indicated. This relation could not be made clear without the results reached in the separate discussions ; with the aid of these, it can be stated very briefly.

In the treatment of the separate themes the object has been to bring out what seemed most essential in regard to each, and to associate with this one or two other aspects of the subject, those being selected that seemed most important and interesting. Thus the study of "The Philosophy of Poetry" is introduced by a consideration of "The Imagination" as the poetic faculty ; and is followed by chapters in regard to certain aspects of nature and life in which poetry has found its most abundant material, and some of its highest inspiration. Under the title of "Duty" the discussion of "The Ultimate Facts of Ethics " is followed by a study of the aspects which duty, in itself at all times the same, is tending to assume at the present day. In the treatment of " The Comic" the two elements — · the primary and the secondary — are presented under the same heading.

CONTENTS.

I. POETRY.

THE IMAGINATION.

THE imagination is in a special sense the poetic faculty. In poetry, indeed, it is subject to certain technical conditions; and it may assume various forms, of which poetry is only one : yet when we regard definiteness of presentation and permanence of result upon the one side, and freedom from physical relations and limitations on the other, poetry may perhaps be regarded as its most characteristic expression. However this may be, the imagination is absolutely essential to poetry of every kind. In considering the nature of poetry, it is therefore important to regard the imagination in the entire range of its activity.

The imagination is the power of mental vision, a power which creates that which it beholds. What might seem, from this statement, to be two acts is really but one. In a dream, for instance, the mind does not create an image, and then perceive it ; the beholding is the creation.

The simplest form of the imagination is that by which the mind reproduces for itself the forms which the senses have presented to it. The captain of a steamer on one of our important coast-lines once told me, that as he steamed along the coast at night he saw constantly passing before him, as if in an unfolding panorama, the scenes near which he was moving. Though all was hidden from the bodily senses, all was open to " the mind's eye." This discerned the whole structure of the coast, hills, forests, and towns, projecting capes and retreating coves ; and by this mental vision the pilot guided, always with success, his vessel's course. It was as when one walks down a familiar street in a thick fog. The houses on either side are not discerned by the eye, but the mind sees them, and the man walks without hesitation or perplexity.

This simple power of reproducing the image of that which has been seen is of more importance than we often think. That is a fine exercise in some schools of art in which an object is shown to the students and then withdrawn, that they may copy it from memory alone. If we could learn to see, to look accurately and take in the real and definite form and color that we see ; and then if we could learn to remember what we have seen, to reproduce it to the eye of the mind as it existed for the eye of the body, life would become a new thing to us. Suppose we could thus recall the forms, the faces, the pictures, the scenes, which we had thus beheld, how would our life be enlarged! If the traveller in Switzerland could bring home in his mind such images of what he has seen, — the peaks, the ranges, the green valleys, the leaping cataracts, the glaciers stretching like seas petrified in a storm, instead of a confused mass of ice and snow, with vague mountains huddled together in shapeless confusion, — how much more worth the while would such a journey be! When shall we learn that the great business of education is not to cram the mind with facts, but to train it to observe, to remember, to think, to deal rightly with all the material that comes to it, and thus to make it the master of itself and of the world? This is the real end of education; and in this the training of the imagination, even in the simple form under which I have defined it, holds no small place.

But this which I have named is only a small part, indeed the smallest part, of the function of the imagination. Not merely does it reproduce for the mind that which the eye has seen ; it goes beyond this. It separates the elements of that which has been beheld, and recombines them in new forms. It goes farther than this. It introduces new elements. It creates for the mind that which the outward senses could not discern. In all this, however, it keeps true to the lessons it has learned. Even where it changes that which has been beheld, even where it introduces new combinations and new elements, it yet holds itself in sympathy with nature, follows her lines, and so works that its results are one with her creations. Thus the poet can write of the temples that the imagination has reared : —

> " And Nature gladly gave them place,
> Adopted them into her race,
> And granted them an equal date
> With Andes and with Ararat."

We may here distinguish between the imagination and the fancy. The imagination follows the lines of nature. Its creations take their place with her works. It brings to light what is hidden in nature, or what she is striving to accomplish. The fancy works more independently. It forsakes the intent of nature and adopts ends of its own. It combines the elements of nature arbitrarily and artificially. Thus the fancy brings together parts of the man and of the horse, and creates the centaur; the imagination creates the Apollo. Fancy creates the dainty Ariel ; imagination creates Miranda with her sweet and innocent wonder. The world of fancy may be beautiful and fascinating, full of airy and delicate shapes ; we find in it enjoyment and refreshment : but it is a world apart from the real world. The world of imagination may be more natural than that of nature herself.

Through this relationship to nature, the imagination may be an aid even in the investigation of science. Professor Tyndall, in that remarkable essay entitled "The Scientific Use of the Imagination," well illustrates this fact.

Science seems cold and hard ; it seems sternly intellectual ; it appears to have to do only with the most solid facts : but yet this science yields itself to the guidance of ·the imagination. Its grandest discoveries, indeed all its grand discoveries, have been made when it has left the region of the seen and the known, and followed the imagination by new paths to regions before unseen.

I here use the term "imagination" to express that insight which anticipates the result of con-

scious analysis and induction, and leaps to conclusions which under its guidance this reasoning
at last attains. The propriety of this use of the
term may appear from the fact that at first the
regions thus laid open are purely imaginary, that
is, they have no recognized reality except that
which the imagination gives to them; and further, from the fact that the insight thus reached
is the result of the constructive power of the
mind. The known and the unknown are combined in a structure which the mind has created
by a single and largely unconscious act. This
act is equally constructive, whether the result
be one that can be represented in pictured form
or not. In either case, it represents a whole
which is the creation of the insight that perceives
it. Such imagination is the inspiration of science, and without it the grandest results of science would not have been attained.

In the essay of which I have spoken, Tyndall
shows how by the aid of the imagination science
reaches the conception, not only of that which
has never been discerned by the senses, but of
that which by its very nature can never be discerned by them. Thus by the aid of the imagination has been reached the conception, the vast-

est which thought in regard to material things
has ever reached, — that of an ethereal substance
stretching farther than the farthest world, clothing the whole boundless universe with light as
with a garment, an infinite ocean whose undulations ripple into light and beauty. The image
of the sea rolling up its pebbly shore furnishes
to the imagination an instrument by which the
movements and effects of this infinite ocean are
made almost visible. These movements and
these results furnish the most interesting and
important elements of our modern science; and
yet this ocean the imagination alone discovered,
it alone has sounded and explored, and it alone
has seen or can see. So, too, are revealed to
us those particles, infinitesimally small, which
we are told give to the heavens their blueness,
and furnish the tints which make the glory of
the evening and the morning sky; those particles which thus are the instruments of much of
the sweetest and sublimest beauty of the world,
but which the essayist to whom I have referred
believes, if they were all swept together so that
the spaces of the heavens should be left blank
and bare, "could all be held in so small a com-
pass as a gentleman's snuff-box." These atoms

must increase mightily, we might almost say infinitely, before they can come within the ken of the most delicate microscope. They are thus the creatures of the imagination, and must always remain her property alone.

The imagination is equally powerful to perceive the relation between objects and elements that before had seemed utterly distinct. Newton, if the old story be true, watching the fall of the apple, began dreaming of the movements of the stars. His imagination leaped to a conception which embraced the universe. Science tried to prove whether this conception were true or not in a body so near us as the moon, and she pronounced it false. Only years later did she acknowledge her mistake, and admit that the imagination was right after all.

The discoveries of science soon become to the minds of most men hard, cold, prosaic facts. We forget that when they first dawned upon the mind of the discoverer they came as poetry. They were the outgrowth of the imagination, which is the poetic faculty, and were surrounded with the glow and the glory of poetry. What vision of the poet by which the sublimities of the heavens offer themselves under some new guise, or make

some new revelation of their inmost nature, is
more worthy the name of poetry, more rouses the
spirit to the enthusiasm of surprise and admiration, than that revelation of the meaning and the
mystery of the lightning - flash which came to
Franklin, whom we are accustomed to regard as
the most prosaic of Americans! When I think
of that familiar picture of the flying kite, the
lowering storm-cloud, and the waiting explorer
full of the sublimity of his dream about the clouds,
and of eagerness to learn whether it would prove
true, it seems to me the triumph of the poetic
element in the world of facts. Or, if we take a
larger and grander illustration, how prosaic
seems to us now the theory of the planetary movements! But what must have been the feeling
of the man upon whom first dawned the thought
that perhaps the earth moves; in whose mind the
thought gathered clearness and definiteness, until
it reached the certainty, the certainty of the intuition of the imagination, that the world does
move! It sometimes seems to me that it must
have been the most thrilling moment in the history of man. This old, solid earth that had been
the one fixed thing in the universe, that had been
the one symbol of the immovable, — this old,

solid earth was torn at last from its moorings, and turned adrift upon the great ocean of space; nay, was sent spinning and whirling through the great vacancy with nothingness above it and beneath. The very foundations of all things were removed. There must have been a sense of homelessness, of eternal wandering, mingled with the joy of the sublimity of the new vision of the ordering of the universe.

If it be thought that these moments of insight and of creation must have been prosaic because they occurred in the midst of the scientific investigation of truth, we must remember that they were moments in which the imagination was supreme, and the imagination is always the same, always full of the glow and the enthusiasm of poetry. But when we say that these discoveries, the discoveries for instance of Newton and Franklin, were the creation of the imagination, we must remember that it was the imagination of Newton and Franklin, of men who had lived in such close sympathy with nature that they could anticipate her revelations, just as two friends may live together so intimately and sympathetically that one can anticipate the words and thoughts of the other. Mere guesses of ordinary men, dreams of mere dreamers, gain no new right and dignity from such triumphs of the imagination which are the play of minds thus trained.

As we look over the world to-day, we find nowhere the imagination more active and eager than in the realms of science. So far, indeed, as science presents itself to the popular apprehension, the imagination seems its ruling spirit. The theory of development, for instance, which is gathering so many facts about itself, which has been so largely accepted by scientific men, — that theory according to which the great barriers by which species and genera are separated, and the different ranks of being are held each in its place, are seen to be removed, and these ranks of being pass one into the other, the lower into the higher, the creeping things standing erect or taking wings, the silent acquiring the gift of song, the dumb the power of speech, the irrational becoming the possessors of genius, — this theory, whether it be true or false, is as really a creation of the mind as the Fables of Æsop, in which the monkey and the fox talk together. The fable may be more fanciful, the theory may be more imaginative. Whether true or false, it fits in with the great lines of nature so as to be worthy of being called a product of the imagination ; but it no more than the fable has any basis of experience. If through the barriers that separate one rank of being from another were ever flung open gate-ways of communication, they were like the doors that in the Arabian tales opened into the solid mountain-side and closed again leaving no scar. If these ranks of being ever rose and moved in glad procession along the upward slope, each passing, by no matter how slow a step, out of its own limitations, and in itself or its posterity entering upon a larger life, it was before the eyes of man were opened to behold. No searching of his awakened powers can detect, even among the remains of an unknown antiquity, any glimpse of the great movement while in process of accomplishment. All, as he looks upon it, is as fixed as the Sphinx that slumbers on the Egyptian sands. All this story of transformation and activity is a dream.

In saying this I would not be understood as implying doubt as to the truth of the system. Indeed, the only pertinence of the reference to it here is found in the assumption of its truth.

In what has been said of the importance of the imagination in scientific research, nothing has been further from my thought than to imply that it may take the place of this. The imagination simply carries a divining-rod, which may suggest in what direction research may be pushed, and it may complete the results of research when this has done its best. It is surprising how little we really see of what we think we see, or hear of what we think we hear. In reading, how few notice a typographical error! How the eye is pained in reading words printed in an unfamiliar alphabet! This is because one has to see distinctly every letter, whereas in the case of the familiar alphabet one takes simply the general impression. The early phonograph, if one knew what it was saying, seemed to speak with absolute distinctness. If one did not know, it was absolutely unintelligible, as the consonants were not sounded. Such illustrations show how the imagination completes the report of the senses, and brings a whole out of fragments. So it completes the work of scientific investigation, and from a few points that have been thus established it constructs some well-rounded theory, which we can hardly realize was not completely bodied forth in them.

I am inclined to think that in the practical af-

fairs of life the imagination fills a place no less
real, if less prominent, than that occupied by it
in the world of science.   Here, however, I must
speak with somewhat less confidence, since, so
far as I know, we have no inside view of the matter from any business man, similar to that which
Professor Tyndall gives in regard to science.   The
position of the imagination would, however, seem
to be somewhat the same in each.   The plodder
in business is the man who goes no farther and
no faster than actual experience would justify.
There is, on the other hand, a genius for affairs
as truly as for science and art.   In every case,
genius works less by a process of conscious reasoning than by the flash of intuition, and less by
abstract conception than by a prophetic beholding of results.   Indeed, the very word "intuition"
signifies a beholding.   Such intuition is, then,
the creative act of the imagination, which, per-
ceiving new relations, forms fresh combinations,
pictures contingencies as really existing and future things as present.   The man lives among
these visions more really than among the actual
things about him.   His investments are guided
by this vision of that which as yet has no substance, and a new fortune is the result.

But here, as before, we must notice that it is in general the imagination of the trained mind that does this work, though here, as everywhere, it is probable that genius may sometimes take the place of training ; but it is the imagination, trained or untrained, and not fancy. The man of fancy also dreams dreams, and risks his money on their truth ; but has left only the memory of his wasted means and of his palaces in the clouds.

Another illustration of the same thing is found in the fact, that after a certain point has been reached the results of business activity possess a value that is largely imaginary. The man does not see his wealth, and from the greater part of it he derives, and can hope to derive, no tangible advantage.

The fact we are considering deserves an important place in our estimate of the world. Truly, as the proverb says, "One half of the world does not know how the other half lives." The poet or the student, living largely in the region of the imagination, wonders how life is possible amid the cold and hard realities of the world. He thinks that life without the play of the imagination would be unendurable. In this he is right. He is wrong in supposing that the

imagination is excluded from these so-called practical affairs. The word "poet," as we all know,
means maker, and every maker, the money-maker
as truly as the maker of statues or of verses,
though in a less degree, is also a maker in the
poetic sense of the word; that is, he is one who
creates by the power of the imagination. The
inventor, the builder, the successful man everywhere, works by the aid of this power. We call
the earth solid. We speak of the hard, unyielding rock; but yet nothing is solid, nothing is
unyielding. Each atom of the firmest rock floats
in an atmosphere of its own. No atom touches
another. They approach one another, and recede
from one another in the whirls of an endless
dance; but they touch one another never. So
we speak of the hard, practical affairs of life,
as though from these were excluded the play
of the imagination, the dream of the poet. But
all the creations of man rest upon the same foundations; they are united by the same cement;
they rest upon and are pervaded by the imagination. This is the creative power of the mind.
It is the vital activity of the mind; and without
it man could not live. It must be admitted that
in business enterprise the imagination is not

manifested in its full beauty. It is limited in its scope. It does not set the spirit free from personal ends. But we must not on this account fail to recognize what it really does accomplish in giving interest and largeness to the life.

I have thus spoken of the imagination as it lends itself to the uses of science and of affairs. I have wished to win confidence for it by showing that even in realms which seem most remote from its true life, it is accepted, under certain conditions, as a guide; that all the grandest results, even in the worlds called unimaginative, are accomplished by its aid. If this is so even in regions where it might seem least at home, must it not be true in what we recognize as the realm more peculiarly its own? Must it not there demand especial confidence?

I know that as the imagination begins to work in a more independent way it is followed by the protests of those who had made glad use of it before. It is looked upon by its former masters as a good servant if well trained. But the question arises, Is this position the only and true position of the imagination? Is it merely a servant? To whom does the world really belong? Is science the mistress of the world? Is business, using the

word to cover all the so called practical enterprises
and occupations of life, — is this the rightful mistress of the world? I would do all honor to those
which rank among the noblest occupations of the
mind; but when they, or the faculties that find
in them scope for their activity, unite to oppress
the imagination, to keep her in a position of servitude, they need not be surprised that she, at
last, asserts her rightful claims.   Though she
be patient and helpful as Cinderella herself, the
time must come when she shall take her true position, and her sisters, that so long have treated
her as their servant, shall be glad to render her
their homage.

For let us ask again, To whom does the world
rightfully belong?   Let us put the matter to a
test.   It is safe to say that the world especially
belongs to the faculty that creates it for us; the
faculty from whose hands we receive it.   Which
faculty thus produces our world?   Let each make
the trial.   The business faculty, I think, will
quietly withdraw from the comparison, however
loudly it may afterward enforce its claims upon
the street.   Let science, then, as representing
the understanding, make the first attempt.   Let
her bring all her methods and appliances; let her

bring her magnificent logic of induction, and let
her furnish to the mind the world that she needs
for her own experiments; or let her even assure
the mind of the existence of this earth. Science
will accept nothing that she cannot demonstrate:
let her demonstrate the reality of the existence
with which she busies herself, and thus let her
prove herself to be the rightful mistress of the
world. The data given her are a few sensations.
Out of these she has to construct the world that
the mind recognizes, or to demonstrate the reality
of this world so that the mind will accept it solely
on the strength of this demonstration. Why does
she not begin? She stands silent and powerless.
Now let the imagination try her power. She has
only a few sensations to work with, the same
material that was offered to her rival. These
are enough for her. She bids the mind look, and
the world stretches before it, the world of mountains and rivers and plains, the world of forests
and cities, the world of science and business.
Where did this world come from? How out of
these few sensations has it been constructed?
Whence comes its roundness, its solidity, its
varied forms, each complete in itself, yet each
helping to form the vast completeness of the

whole? How was the sudden transformation wrought? I cannot tell you. I only know that it is the work of the imagination. She touched these few sensations and they became the world, the world of strength, of life, of beauty, which the mind, moved by its own instinctive faiths, accepts as a reality so soon as it is looked upon.

Shall we say that the imagination is so akin to the creative Power of the universe that the mind feels that her creation is one with that of this infinite Power, and thus accepts it in the place of that? However this may be, the world as it exists for us is the creation of the imagination, and we accept it at her hands. This fact has been recognized by the most profound philosophies. The power which created for us the world of sensation and perception Kant and Fichte unite in calling the Productive Imagination.

If the imagination created the world, we must admit that it belongs to her. She is its queen by virtue of this right. She lends it to science to analyze, to study, to reason about. She lends it to business to work with, or to play with, whichever word we choose to take. She loves to see her world thus occupied. She plays the part of a genial and helpful hostess. She will lead science in her explorations through regions that she knows well, because they are her own. She will guide and suggest and be as helpful as she can. She will whisper to business, and hint where her treasures lie. But when, because she is thus helpful, she is regarded as a servant only, and her guests begin to lord it over her, and she is treated as the airy Ariel was treated, only the service to which she is held is to be perpetual, then she may well assert her right of sovereignty.

Thus the test we choose decides between the conflicting claims. It is like the slipper of glass which, fitting the delicate foot of Cinderella, proved her the prince's chosen bride. But, not content with this mere demonstration, the maiden of the story pulled the other slipper from her pocket, and then at the god-mother's fairy touch, stood arrayed in the splendor that befitted her estate. Thus the imagination, from the mere demonstration of her rights, passes to the hardly needed, though welcome, illustration of them. She further shows her creative power by completing the structure which had been left unfinished. Art and poetry are methods or instruments of the imagination, and these complete the world. The forms of life as we see them are not perfect.

Life as we see it is not perfect.   It may be pressing forward towards perfection, but the perfection is not yet attained.   Further, the perfection
that the world has cannot fully manifest itself.
Art puts the finishing touch to this which has
been left incomplete.   It gives us the ideal man,
the ideal life, the ideal nature.   As we look upon
them we feel that this is the real man, the real
life, the real nature.   The imagination has brought
to light the mystery of the world.   She has placed
before us that up towards which nature was striving, that without which nature is incomplete,
that which is thus the reality of nature.   The
men that we see are not the true men.   The true
man we find in the Apollo of the Vatican.   Indeed, we do not see men.   We see about us forms
which represent men ; but their deep inner life
is hidden from us.   If we would really see men
we must turn to Shakespeare.   So, too, the perfect life to which the moralist and the philanthro-
pist would point us is the ideal life.   It is as yet
largely a dream-life.   It is the goal of humanity.
Its reality and its glory are the explanation, because they are the stimulus, of the struggles of
humanity ; but as yet they are, in their fulness,
the possession of the imagination only.   If once

the ideal life actually trod, in living shape, the earth, we have now to reconstruct it for ourselves, by the help of the imagination, out of the few shining fragments that remain.

Thus does the imagination further prove her right to the world by the completion of it. It is as when Virgil would prove his ownership of the poem which he had formed, by placing upon the wall the riddle of the unfinished lines. Thus does imagination prove her ownership by her completion of her work.

Another illustration of the position which the imagination holds in the world may be found in the permanency of the results which are specially due to her power. Works of science, of philosophy, treatises on practical matters, and nearly all productions of a kindred nature, in time become obsolete. They either lose their value or are valuable only as helps in constructing the history of their time. But a genuine product of the imagination, whether in literature or art, has an eternal value. It is as fresh at the end of centuries as at the time of its creation. The ancient Aryan, standing at the very beginning of history, felt the beauty of the Dawn, and uttered this sense of beauty in hymns which thrill us now across all these thousands of years. Greek art and poetry

are as fresh to-day as the works of our contemporaries ; fresher, indeed, so far as they are more
beautiful than they. If any system of philosophy retains its youth as the works of the imagination retain theirs, it is because it is akin to
them. The philosophy of Plato rests upon the
imagination. It is in its essence poetry. It rests
upon the assumption that the ideal is more real
than the actual. The actual things about us are
only the imperfect images, the fleeting shadows
of the ideal things which only the soul sees, and
which alone are eternal. It is this element in the
works of Plato which has made them a perennial
source of joy and inspiration.

I suppose that the reason why the works of the
imagination are thus enduring, why beauty is
thus immortal, is that here something is completed. Something has reached a perfect issue,
and here the creative power of the universe may
pause. Everything else is in process. Systems,
plans, theories, hurry on one after the other.
Knowledge becomes lost in larger knowledge.
Nothing is an end in itself, but that in which
some ideal of the soul has assumed perfect form.
That object in which this has been accomplished
is taken out of the whirl of things, and set apart
in its completeness to rest in immortal youth.

THE IMAGINATION (*continued*).

WE are now ready to compare the imagination with the faculty of the mind that is most distinctly opposed to it. This antithetical faculty is the understanding. The understanding represents the mind in its analytical activity, as the imagination represents it in its constructive activity. Practically, analysis is for the most part connected to a greater or less degree with synthesis. We can, however, abstract it from all connection of the sort, and consider it purely in itself. The understanding, then, gives us the details of prose; the imagination gives us the fulness and unity of poetry. The understanding thus claims to give us the actual ; the imagination gives us the ideal. The understanding, tearing the world apart, analyzing it into its ultimate particles, gives us the poor fragments that remain as its equivalent ; the imagination rests content with nothing less than the rounded beauty of the whole. Which of these is nearer right ?

You examine a painting with a microscope and report all that you can find. You analyze it into its approximate elements, and discover the oil and the lead and the canvas, and whatever else entered into its material structure. These elements you give to us and say, Here is your picture of which you made so much account; you see all that there was of it, a little canvas, a little lead, a little oil. But have we here all the elements of the painting? Was there not something else? Was there not something that fled before the analysis of the understanding, something even that the microscope could not discern? Was there not present the ideal which exists for the imagination only, the ideal which used these poor elements and gave them all their worth? This ideal has a reality independent of that of the medium through which it manifests itself. It existed before it used this material; it exists after the material has been destroyed. It may use other material for its manifestation. The perfect pictures of Raphael are copied in stone upon the walls of St. Peter's. If the ideal is as perfectly represented as before, nothing is lost by the change. The substance, the reality of the picture may be thus transferred, and does this ideal go for nothing? Shall we accept as the equivalent of our painting, as the reality of it, anything that leaves this out of the account?'

And yet this is the way in which many at the present day would treat the world. There is a tendency, more or less pronounced, to explain everything from below upwards; to place the emphasis on physical facts and relations. I would not speak slightingly of the service which the investigations and theories of science have rendered to the world. I would, indeed, join in the acclaim with which such service has been received. It is only against the neglect of elements, of which such investigations and theories would make small account, that I would protest. This protest is not aimed against physical science itself; this is doing nobly its special work. It is aimed at the error of taking the results of physical science as if they contained the whole truth, or even the most important elements of truth.

I believe all that the botanist tells me about the flower. I follow with intense interest his analysis. But if he sees in the flower nothing more than his analysis can show him, then the little child that claps its hands in delight at the beauty of the first blossom of the spring sees the flower more truly than he does. I believe all that the anatomist tells me of the structure of the human body. His study of bone and muscle, of nerve and artery, brings to light facts of wonderful interest. But if he finds in man nothing but what his study of anatomy can reveal, then the little child that rests in sweet trustfulness in its mother's arms is nearer to the truth of things than he is. The Buddhist saw in man only a walking skeleton. Behind the fairest smile he saw only the grinning skull. This is not a cheerful view of life ; neither is it the true view.

There is something in the universe which the scalpel and the retort cannot discover. The whole is more than the sum of its parts. The whole is more real than its parts. The ideal is more real than the actual. In this Plato was right. The ideal is a greater power in the universe than the actual. It destroys the actual that it may fulfil itself. The oak which the little sapling is to become is more real than it, for the little sapling yields to its power and becomes the oak. If the theory of development be the truth, then, far back in the ages, when the earth swarmed with reptiles, and later, when creatures more perfect to a large extent replaced these, through all this succession of forms the ideal man, though non-existing, was yet more real than they; for, pressing on through all of these, he transformed them more and more into his own likeness, until at last he stood forth in his true nobility. These lower forms were but the masquerading garments of the real presence and power that were hidden in them. So to-day, as in all periods of human history, the ideal state is more real than the existing state. We know that it is, because it shatters the existing state into fragments, or transforms it by slow degrees into itself. Thus hath God chosen the things which are not, to bring to nought things that are.

There is in nature and in life an infinite fulness which escapes the analysis of the understanding. If you doubt this, look abroad over the earth. What is the ocean? The chemist will tell you what it is. It is water containing in solution a certain proportion of salt and of other elements. Such is the ocean. This is all that any analysis can find in it. But what and whence is its beauty, its sublimity? We have already seen what constitutes the blue of the heavens. We have in imagination gathered in a single snuff-

box the points of matter with which the depths
of space are strown ; against which the minute
undulations of an invisible ether dash, and thus
produce the blueness of the sky. This is all won-
derfully interesting. It gives a possible explanation of the blueness of the heavens ; it gives no
hint of an explanation of their divine beauty.

I call the power of apprehending beauty that
of the imagination, because it is a manifestation
of the constructive intuition of the soul. The
unity of the object found beautiful is not in itself, except as some power akin to that which
finds it there embodied it in the material atoms
which make up the outward reality. If I enjoy
the beauty of a picture, I, so far as I am able, reconstruct the ideal which inspired the artist and
presided over his work.

Beauty represents, the wholeness, the life, the
ideal element of the world. This the imagination
lays hold of. The understanding cannot grasp
it, because no material analysis can reach it. It
is interesting to see the straits to which men are
reduced, who feel the power of beauty in the outer
world, who are thus forced to recognize its presence, but who yet would be loyal to the understanding only. Tyndall has an imagination as

keen as that of any poet, an imagination which continually finds in the most delicate and truthful phrases of the purest poets its best utterance. He loves the mountains. He loves to climb their snowy sides. Difficulties only inspire him. His labor is its own great reward. But as he enjoys this play of the physical nature, — for to his athletic frame this toil is only play, — he is conscious of a joy that is not merely that of the physical exertion ; a joy that comes to him from the mountains. In some way they have a power over him. They thrill and exalt his spirit. He is a philosopher and he will explain this. Or rather he is a man of science and as such loyal to the understanding. The companions of his studies are men of science ; most of them more purely men of the understanding than he, men in whom the imagination has less place. He would justify to them and to himself this unscientific enthusiasm for the beauty of the Alps. His mind is too sharp and logical to be imposed upon by any theory which would make this enjoyment the result of association from his earlier years ; for he tells us that as a boy he loved nature. He falls back to " the forgotten associations of a far-gone ancestry," and regards these as probably the most "potent elements in the feeling." He here rejects one element and accepts the other of Herbert Spencer's explanation of the peculiar enjoyment of natural scenery. The first element, that which results from our own early associations, we must with Tyndall reject as an explanation of the mystery. It is a mistake to say that in general our appreciation of natural scenery grows with our growing years. Professor Tyndall, as we have seen, loved nature as a boy. Wordsworth cries : —

> "My heart leaps up when I behold
> A rainbow in the sky.
> So was it when my life began,
> So is it now I am a man."

The poet was fortunate that he could add this last line ; for too often the love of the beautiful fades out of the mind as years go on. Elsewhere Wordsworth himself tells us that even for him there had "passed a glory from the earth." Men have confessed, even in the presence of Niagara, that the fall of some little stream had more power to move them in their youth than the sublimity of this mighty cataract had in their maturity. If we lived aright, perhaps this would never be so. As we do live, it is the case too often. This shows at least that these early associations are not the prime elements of enjoyment.

But how is it with the forgotten associations of a far-gone ancestry? These forgotten associations of an unknown ancestry form now the stronghold of the so-called experience-philosophy. It draws not only from the associations of human ancestors which have become embodied in the brains of their descendants, but upon those of a succession almost infinite of the lower types of creation out from which the human type has been by slow degrees evolved. When a system retreats to such strongholds as this, and loses itself in such mazy labyrinths, it may well feel secure. But I think that the case in which Professor Tyndall falls back upon the theory, furnishes a test of its truth or falsity more accurate than we could have expected.

Before applying this test, however, we may pause for a moment to notice the contrast between the careful methods that men of science use in matters that belong to the physical world, and the frequent looseness of their reasoning as soon as they enter the realm of philosophy. It would sometimes seem as if they fancied that here all is guess-work, and that one guess is as

good as another.   There is, for instance, a style
of reasoning often called the *Post hoc ergo propter
hoc* argument.   It is to the effect that if one event
is seen to follow another it must be the result of
it.   A man takes a medicine and gets well ; therefore, he argues, the medicine cured him.   The
savages shout and make all the noise they can
during an eclipse.   This has always been done
within the memory of man, and the eclipse has
always come to an end : what more could they
want to prove that the outcry put an end to the
eclipse ?   This kind of reasoning is not in very
good repute among scientific men, and methods
have been devised by which such looseness of
thought may be avoided.   One of these is called
"the method of difference."   It asks whether
the fact to be explained ever occurs apart from
that other fact which is assumed to be its cause.
If it does, it is obvious that the assumption is
false.   Now, in the theory to which we have referred, Mr. Spencer uses, and Professor Tyndall
cheerfully accepts, an argument of the simplest
Post hoc ergo propter hoc order.   Wordsworth
drew inspiration from the presence of nature ;
his savage ancestors once hunted and fished in
the wilderness : what could be more obvious than

that we have here effect and cause? We can only regret that Wordsworth lived before this important discovery had been made. It might have modified some of his poems essentially. In his simplicity he sang : —

> " I have felt
> A presence that disturbs me with the joy
> Of elevated thoughts ; a sense sublime
> Of something far more deeply interfused,
> Whose dwelling is the light of setting suns,
> And the round ocean, and the living air,
> And the blue sky, and in the mind of man ;
> A motion and a spirit that impels
> All thinking things, all objects of all thoughts,
> And rolls through all things.   Therefore am I still
> A lover of the meadows and the woods
> And mountains. "

Perhaps it is not too late to re-shape these lines. All that is necessary is to amend by striking out all before the " therefore," and inserting a statement more in harmony with the phase of modern thought that we are considering.   Let us make the experiment : —

> *My savage fathers in the forest depths*
> *Once lurked for foes and hunted for their game ;*
> *And in the forest streams they caught their fish.*
> *Such was their life, and* " therefore am I still
> A lover of the meadows and the woods
> And mountains."

But I fear that, if an adaptation of Sydney Smith's joke may be allowed, we shall be accused of " making game " of the object of the poet's enthusiasm. Let us, first of all, be sure that the theory is correct. Let us do what Professor Tyndall would be the first to do in any matter of physical science, — apply the " method of difference." The circumstances under which Professor Tyndall refers to this theory furnish a most admirable opportunity for this application. The great beauty of the Alps which stirred his soul burst upon him most fully when he stood on heights almost inaccessible, amid ice and snow, where even the scanty mountain herbage did not follow him. When he stood surrounded thus by the lonely and waste sublimities of nature, then it was that his soul was most filled with the glory of the scene. This experience is a common one. For myself, I have never felt the beauty of the outward world more than in the region of Zermatt, in Switzerland. Upon the Gorner Grat one stands in the midst of snow mountains that are gathered as if in a mighty conclave. One shrinks, as if one were intruding unbidden into the council chamber of these monarchs of the earth. On one side they press near to the spec-

tator ; on the other they stretch far away, one
rising beyond the other. From each mountain
descends a glacier. These, uniting in the valley,
form one mighty glacier which stretches around
the foot of the central mountain upon which we
stand, — a mountain which seems in the comparison but a lowly hill. Thus we stand in the
midst of the solitudes of nature. There is no
life anywhere, only the magnificence of snow and
ice and rocky precipices. Or, from a different
point of view, by the "Black Lake" and the
Schmutzthal, one sees some of the same mountains, — Monte Rosa and the towering sharpness
of the Matterhorn. If before we felt in the presence of a mighty conclave, we see now the same
potentates, only each seems withdrawn to his
own estate, and lordlier in his isolation than
when gathered with his peers in lofty council.

Now no theory of the power which natural
scenery has over us is complete that does not
take into account the delight that we experience
in spots like these. The theory of Spencer that
I have referred to does not do this. I am sure
that none of our savage ancestors ever found
their joy among wildernesses of ice and snow.
Thus no associations of antiquity, however remote

and dim, could be stirring in our heart.   Indeed,
the frozen regions of the North have sometimes
been considered, as by the ancient Iranians, to be
the abode of the powers of evil.   In order to
settle the question as to the possibility of the
spontaneous origin of the lowest forms of life, a
vessel, sealed closely so that no germs from the
outer air can reach the liquid with which it is
filled, is subjected to heat so intense as to kill
whatever germs may be already existing in the
liquid.   If, after this, living forms are found in it,
the inference is that they have had an independent or spontaneous origin.   With the results of
such experiments, and the accuracy with which
they have been performed, we have here nothing
to do ; but it appears to me that in the case
which we are considering, that of the special enjoyment of beauty among the glaciers of the
high Alps, cold performs the part which heat was
designed to perform in the experiment of the
germ-producing liquid.   The possibility of any
historical association of the kind that the theory
demands is frozen out.

Other natural scenes which we enjoy most
keenly stand in a similar relation to the history of
the race.   The spectacle of the sea in a storm is

one of the most inspiring that nature can afford. Our savage ancestors had in part their play as well as their work in the waters of the quiet sea; but never their sport, and never if possible their work, on the sea when it was tossed by the tempest. There are other scenes of nature, which we recognize as beautiful, to which our savage ancestors could have stood in no different relations from those in which we stand to-day. What ancestor of ours ever coasted down the rainbow, or played hide-and-seek among the stars?

But the association, even where it may exist, is not competent to account for the result. One whose ancestors have lived in certain regions, or under certain circumstances, may feel a pleasure when he finds himself in the same regions, or under similar circumstances; but this does not explain the exaltation, the inspiration, the spiritual power, of the beauties and sublimities of nature. Of the grandeur of the mountain scenery Professor Tyndall himself exclaims that "half the interest in such cases is psychological; the soul takes the hint of surrounding nature and becomes majestic." Such psychological inspiration could not be derived from any inherited association with merely animal enjoyment. If it is inherited at all, it is because our ancestors were spiritual as well as animal, because their hearts thrilled at the vision of the beautiful as ours do. Indeed, far back as history extends we find this sense of the beautiful, of the grand, of the inspiring.

> " So was it when my life began,
>   So is it now I am a man,"

sings the poet, and the race can take up and echo back the song : —

> " So was it when my life began."

The Aryan hymns to the Dawn show a sense of beauty as keen at least as that which we possess to-day. The mythologies, the religions, of the world, have sprung largely out of this sense. Our early ancestors felt the glory of the heavens, the beauty and mystery of the forest depths. They felt this strange, inspiring, awing, and uplifting power in nature. They felt it and they called it God. The early Aryan praise of the beauty of the dawning was a hymn.

We thus reach the culmination of our theme. We have seen in the imagination simply the imaging or the reflecting power of the mind; then we have seen in it the guide and the inspiration of science and of life; then, after considering its primacy among our faculties as being the power which bestows upon us the world itself, we have followed it in its freer and more normal activity, and seen in it the idealizing faculty, that which evolves out of nature and finds in nature the ideal element which is its reality. This ideal element manifests itself in beauty; and now we reach the point where it manifests itself in religion.

I can conceive that some, who have followed with sympathy the discussion thus far, may here become repelled. They may protest against that use of the word "imagination" by which it is applied to the discernment of the Divine Presence in nature. Here is no image, they would say. The very meaning of the experience is the being brought face to face with that which is invisible, with that which reveals itself through all forms, but which itself is beyond any form. They would prefer some other term. They would speak, perhaps, of the "idealizing power of the mind" instead of the "imagination." So far as the literal signification of words is concerned, the substitution that I have suggested would help little. The word "idea" etymologically means something that is seen. It implies an image no less really than the word which it would supplant. I do not care, however, to rest the justification of my use of the word "imagination" upon any such etymological and remote consideration as that which has just been named. It is in part because the word "idea" has to so large an extent lost its primitive force, and has acquired a purely abstract meaning, that I would prefer the other. There is a beholding that is with the eyes of the spirit alone. There is an imaging that involves no limit of corporeal form. Such a beholding is the discernment of the Divine Presence in the world; such an imaging is the gathering up out of the manifoldness of nature the scattered manifestations of this Presence, and blending them into a sublime oneness. Chiefly, however, I prefer to use in this connection the word "imagination," because it indicates that the activity which it would name is the same that we have traced under lower forms. The power that constructs, out of the elements which the botanist would separate, the ideal unity of the flower, and rejoices in the beauty which becomes thus manifest to it, is akin to that which constructs the ideal unity of the universe, and worships the divine splendor which shines forth from this.

A very instructive lesson on the relation between the imagination and religion is found in the life of Darwin. Through the absorbing interest which his scientific investigations had for him, we are told, his æsthetic sense and his religious sense became weakened together. He lost his taste for poetry, pictures, and music, just as he lost the power of religious faith and emotion. I would not be understood as implying that an æsthetic taste is essential if religion is to exist. Unhappy would it be for the world if this were the case. In a complete religion there exists, however, a relation between the two. The æsthetic taste is the most natural and ordinary expression of the imagination ; and the imagination, as we have seen, is one with that power of constructive vision by which man finds himself face to face with the Divine Presence that glorifies the world. In the case of Darwin, had the religious sense alone been dulled, there are some who would have seen in the fact an evidence of the worthlessness of this sense. They would have seen a legitimate triumph of science over what they would call superstition. There are few, however, who would not recognize the fact that the, dying out of the sense of beauty from any

life is a real loss. There are few who do not realize that the enjoyment of beauty is one of the
normal functions of the soul; and that it cannot
fail without disturbing the integrity of the life.
The fact that it and the sense of the reality of
religion together faded out of the life of Darwin
may perhaps help some to realize that possibly
the latter might also have been a real loss; that
the capacity for religious emotion may perhaps
also be one of the normal elements of the mind.

In our thought of God are blended the loftiest
ideals of the soul. We find hints of the presence
of God in the universe, but hints only. The as-
tronomer tells us that he has swept the heavens
with his telescope and found no God. Only "the
vision and the faculty divine;" only the imagination, which is the eye of the soul, which is the
culmination and representative of its faculties, —
only this shows us God. We receive Him through
the imagination, just as we receive the outward
world through the imagination. Religion is
poetry believed in, just as the outward world is
poetry believed in; and when poetry is true, it is
truer than anything beside. The conception of
each is reached in the same way, and each demands a like faith. Thus the imagination, first

the explorer and then the poet of the race, becomes at last its seer, its prophet, and its priest.
The senses give us only a confused series of sensations. The understanding gives us only lifeless fragments. The imagination gives us the
universe in its wholeness, and transforms it into
the living garments of Divinity.

Here our investigation must reach its close.
We have followed it far enough, however, to be
sure of one practical result. If the imagination
is thus important, a complete education should
give a prominent place to studies in which the
imagination shall find the special culture and
stimulus that it needs ; and for this a mere scientific training, however important it may be, is not
enough. I may be reminded, indeed, of the part
which, as we have seen, the imagination plays in
scientific progress ; and it may be urged that thus
science alone may give to the imagination all the
scope and stimulus which it requires. But it
must be remembered that while a high order of
imagination is needed to make the discoveries
which are the glory of science, only a low order
of imagination is absolutely needed to accept
them. They appear to their discoverers first in
the form of poetry ; but after they have been

announced and accepted, they enter into the mass
of the truisms of the race, and are learned as
prose. Thus the point that I am urging may
appear more obvious and important than before.
For if the imagination fails to receive the development which it needs, not only will those high
truths which seem more directly dependent upon
it tend to become dim and disappear, but science itself will lose that mighty impulse which
has been the moving power in its advance, and
its grand career of triumph will reach its end.

In the examination and comparison through
which we have passed, I may seem to some to
have spoken slightingly of the scientific methods
and results of the present day. I must, in conclusion, once again protest against any such in-
terpretation of my words. If I honor anything in
the present age, it is the spirit of scientific investigation. I accept with delight its revelations. It
is only when it claims that its methods and its
results exhaust the universe that we must remind
it that it stands on borrowed ground; that we
must point out its limitations; that we must fall
back upon the soul, — the soul with its faith and
its aspiration, with its ideals, with its creative
power which is akin to the creative power of
God.

We must remember that there is hardly one among the truly representative men of modern science who does not recognize, more or less timidly or confidently, something of this reality which is vaster than any possible reach of what we call science; who does not thus recognize something of the world of imagination. Herbert Spencer sees the knowable as wrapped in by the unknowable, the finite by the absolute. How did he reach this thought? This unknowable, this absolute, — his senses have not discerned it. No reasoning can establish it. Only the imagination has revealed it to him. He trusts her so far. He lets her construct the heavens which shall wrap in his little earth. But there he bids her stay her hand. No color shall she introduce into these outspread heavens; no delicate noonday blue, no glow of morning, shall she paint there. She may not light there the eternal stars which shall illuminate its darkness. If she streak this darkened heaven with any hint of a coming dawn, it is done against his protest, and the result remains because unrecognized. He trusts her for the greater; why should he not trust her for the less?

But even did we find in our scientific men no

recognition of anything beyond the results of science itself, in the narrowest acceptation of the word, should we even then strive to check its march? Should we look at the results of its analysis, at the elements which it gives us in the place of the living universe, and cry in our despair —

> " Woe ! woe ! Thou hast destroyed it,
> The beautiful world " ?

Nay, rather we should recognize its ministry and accept its service. The imagination, the discerning and creative power of the soul, should rouse itself to a higher work. It should fill out these elements with its own life. Mr. Ruskin would have the painter know nothing of anatomy. The study of the bones of the arm, he believes, will prevent him from constructing with grace the picture of the arm. But suppose the knowledge of the anatomy of the arm to be so familiar as to become a part of the mind itself, and the imagination so powerful that it can use this knowledge without being hampered by it. In this case we should have both accuracy and grace. So should the imagination master the results of science. If it does this, it will find that it has gained infinitely through that which it most dreaded.

The child draws sweet music from its little pipe. Then comes the organ-builder, with his wilderness of material. He makes a vast machine, and calls to his aid, it may be, the power of steam to move the ponderous machinery. And shall this machine, we cry, take the place of the pipe which the child filled with its breath and modulated with its fingers? But wait till the organist takes his seat, and then say whether you have gained or lost by the exchange. So the poet asks with indignant remonstrance. "In the place of the living universe will science give us this huge machine?" But here also wait for the final judgment till the master-player shall appear.

THE PHILOSOPHY OF POETRY.

WHILE the imagination, as we have seen, makes its power felt in almost every sphere of life, its most distinctive and generally recognized manifestation is in what are known as "the fine arts." Poetry, if not the greatest of these arts, is in some respects the most interesting. It is the most important of those arts the masterpieces of which any one of us can always have at hand. We must travel far to meet Raphael and Michael Angelo. Homer and Shakespeare come to us. Further, there is no other art that has at its command such varied material. This being so, it is a little singular that the definitions of poetry are for the most part so unsatisfactory. A definition that has been repeated by various English authors makes poetry to be "the language of passion or imagination formed into regular numbers." This definition is substantially given by Blair, Hazlitt, and others. It is obviously no definition, for it lacks unity. It gives two species with no genus : the poetry of imagination and that of passion, with nothing to unite them except the metrical form.

Aristotle almost says what he has sometimes been reported as saying, that all poetry is imitation. On the other hand, Milton, in a phrase often quoted of late, insists, among other things, that poetry should be impassioned. His full statement is that poetry should be "simple, sensuous, and impassioned." The definition is a striking one. Elsewhere I may refer to the two specifications that are first named in it. For the present I wish to emphasize merely the last.

There is a singular contrast between this definition and the one that was just before quoted in connection with Aristotle. The one would make poetry to be passion, the other would make it to be imitation. Imitation implies unreality so far as the definite content is concerned. Passion implies the most intense reality. Here we have over against one another the two elements, imagination and passion, that were brought loosely together in the first definition that was named.

I have dwelt on the two definitions last given because I accept them both. It will be in part my object to illustrate and reconcile them.

Poetry is too often discussed as if it were something by itself, to be considered apart from anything else. Poetry is the species of a genus. It
is a branch of art. It is distinguished from other
branches of art by the nature of its material,
which is language, and by all that is involved in
this. Further, art itself is not an ultimate. It is
one of the forms under which beauty is manifested. Before asking the nature of poetry we
must gather from the nature of beauty in general,
and that of art in particular, certain principles
which we may apply to it. I must then ask the
patience of the reader, while I seem to turn for a
while from our proper theme, since only in this
way can we obtain any true basis for our judgment of it. The statement of these general
principles will indeed occupy the larger part of
this discussion. When they are once established,
they can be easily and briefly applied.

We have first to establish certain principles in
regard to beauty in general. The first principle
to be affirmed in regard to beauty concerns its
content; that is, we have to determine the nature of the material that is included in the general term "beautiful."

Every form of being, when distinctly presented

to us, is beautiful. In this the crudest "realism" is right. As we ordinarily stand related to the world, however, few forms of being are distinctly presented to us. One form of being encroaches upon another, and represses or distorts it. Thus realism itself, rightly understood, would drive us to "idealism," in the true meaning of the word. Thus, in the judgment of the best thinkers, beauty is found in the manifestation of the idea; in the Platonic sense of the term. In more ordinary speech, beauty is the manifestation of the ideal or typical.

This may be illustrated by the charm of music. In music we have the ideal sound. Under ordinary circumstances the sound is a chance product depending on the relations of things that exist without regard to it. Under these circumstances sound exists, for the most part, simply as noise. In the case of music, the instruments exist for the sake of the sound, and conform themselves to its laws. Thus in music we have tones in the place of noise. The tone is the ideal sound. By this I mean that in the tone the undulations from which the sound springs are so arranged as to produce continuity ; or if we have several series of undulations at the same time, they are so arranged as to blend and to produce a single effect, giving us a unity that is compound and organic. In each case we have a unity of result: in the one, that of the continuance of the same tone; in the other, that of combination, which also has a certain continuance. In mere noise sound is broken up into disconnected and often discordant elements. Some form of unity is needed for any 'impression that shall be really characteristic of its cause, and thus it is that through the musical tone one is brought into relation with sound itself, as one is not through a noise, let it be ever so deafening. What is here said refers, of course, only to the satisfaction that comes from the material element of music; and not at all to the other ideals that may be expressed through it.

From this example we can understand the meaning of a characteristic of beauty that is often insisted upon; namely, that it requires unity in variety. It is not that the mere perception of unity in variety gives a sense of beauty. It is that without variety there can be no material to affect us; and unless the elements are concentrated in such a way that a single effect is produced, we can get no characteristic impression from them. A loadstone is powerless till you

have found its poles ; and there could be no poles
without mass.   Such is the nature of the unity in
variety which is required for any form of beauty.

In the world of organic life, also, the beautiful
is that which is typical.   This statement does not
refer to that form of life which is most typical of
the species to which it may belong.   It must not
be understood that the typical frog, or the typical
hippopotamus, must, according to this view, be
beautiful.   The type which is beautiful is not
that of the species or the genus, but of that form
of being which these represent.   That living
thing is most beautiful which best manifests life ;
while that in which the presence of life is most
obscured will be the opposite of beautiful.   " So
we exterminate the deer," exclaims Thoreau,
" and substitute the hog."   The hog is here contrasted with the deer, as the prosaic with the
beautiful ; and the two may serve to illustrate the
point which we are considering.   The wild boar,
indeed, long, lank, and terrible in its fierceness,
has a certain picturesqueness, at least, in its
native wilds ; but from the fatted hog this picturesqueness has departed.   The hog, we say, is
gross looking.   By this we mean that in it life
seems lost in matter.   It seems less like a living

organism than it does like a piece of awkward carpentry. It is such a shape as a boy might whittle out with his jackknife. Its cylindrical body is without longitudinal curves. At one extremity it falls off in a clumsy approach to something like a point. To the other is abruptly attached a slight curl. Whatever vital expression might come to it from eyes and mouth is lost in the puffed and swollen aspect that constitutes its whole face. Its expression is not animal, it is worse. It is that of gluttony and weak sensualism. When we say this we must remember that the sensualism which the expression of the fatted hog suggests is not that of its gluttony but of ours. The deer, on the other hand, displays the presence of life at every point. All the members of the organism flow together in graceful curves. There is nothing mechanical ; there is no carpenter's work. There is simply the presence of life which has created and which animates the whole.

We thus see one of the aspects of the human form which makes it, when graceful and beautiful, more perfect than any other. The quadruped in standing depends largely on mechanical support. The horse can sleep on his feet almost as well as if lying down. With man this is different. He stands by vital power more than by mechanical. The muscles of all parts of the body contribute to the preservation of his poise.

Even animals that commonly are ungainly sometimes surprise us with their grace. The kangaroo had always seemed to me awkward and ill-proportioned; but once I saw one startled into a beauty equal to that of the stag. The body assumed a graceful poise; the ears and the delicate head were animated and intent. Commodore Porter relates a scene in which Lincoln, if I may name him in this connection, was animated by an unwonted passion, and he describes him as becoming positively handsome. In such cases it is a fresh influx of life that takes possession of the organism and manifests itself in every part.

More important, however, than the life of the individual is the life of the whole. Nature forms the background of all special existences, and is present in them as well as about them. The forces of nature, when they are really displayed, always give us the sense of beauty. It is obvious that we may sometimes have in this way a collision between the different kinds of beauty. The forces of nature must display themselves by their effects. The action of wind and wave may be exhibited by the repression of organic completeness. Thus imperfection may often be more beautiful than perfection. The beauty of nature may be marred by any object that seems to stand out too conspicuously and inharmoniously over against it. We see, thus, that the assertion so often made, that beauty consists in perfection, however true when rightly understood, is subject to many qualifications. A ruin may seem more beautiful than the perfect structure ever did. The ruin has become a part of the natural world. The building no longer stands out in its self-assertion against the face of nature. Its conceit is gone. Thus an abbey in ruins, when enough remains of pillar and arch to suggest the grace of man's handiwork, is more beautiful than it was in its fresh completeness. We no longer see it, we see nature in it. We can thus understand how rudeness may have a charm to which finished grace cannot attain. The skilfully modelled clipper seems designed to rule the waves. It seems something over against them, a foreign body that has come to dominate them. A clumsy Dutch vessel, which from the point of view of the sailor is little better than a tub, may be more picturesque than the clipper with all its delicacy of curve and sharpness of prow. So too an animal that is awkward or horrible when seen by itself, may help to make a scene of beauty when beheld in his natural environment, in which all the elements are in harmony, as a serpent hanging from a tree in a tropical forest.

Above the beauty of sound and color and form is the beauty of spirit. In the spiritual world a wholly new realm is open to us, which repeats, only on a higher plane, the relations which moved our hearts in the world of nature and of life. Here also there are storms and calms; here also there are grace and strength. There is the world of the emotions and the passions. There are love and joy, and sorrow and fear.

Above the world of the passions there is the world of thought. This is not in itself beautiful. It is the result of abstraction from all the lower forms of existence. If it is to be an object of beauty, it must become embodied in such a way that it shall appear in living presence before us. We have here the world of ideas, in the everyday meaning of that term. These ideas must be in some sort transformed into ideals in order to enter the world of beauty. They must, to use the word of Milton, become sensuous.

We have thus indicated the elements through which beauty may be manifested. We find they include all the realms of nature, life, or spirit. We have, at the same time, a test by which we may distinguish, at least in part, what is not beautiful from that which is. That is not beautiful in which the form of existence, that is the object of contemplation, is in any way repressed or degraded. If life is the thing that is manifested, the life must be free and whole. In the world of spirit there must be neither brutality nor weakness. Such imperfections, if they are present, must tend to the exaltation and the intensifying of that which is perfect, according to some other type ; or by contrast and occasion in some other aspect of the type to which they belong.

We have thus a theory of beauty which lends itself to all the varied forms of existence that fill the universe, and to the universe itself, could we rise to the contemplation of it. The theory is as delicate and universal in its application as beauty itself. Indeed it is less a theory of beauty than a statement of the conditions on which, as experience teaches us, beauty depends.

If we look beyond these to some inner relationship between the external world and ourselves, through which the joy of beauty comes to us under these circumstances, we should say that we are so one with the world about us that we have a sense of freedom in its freedom and of life in its life.[1]

The second statement that we have to make in regard to beauty naturally results from the first. It concerns its form, as that its content. If beauty is the manifestation of the ideal, then it is for contemplation alone. This also is a matter in regard to which the best scholars agree. If beauty is a matter of contemplation only, then all other ends and uses are excluded from it, and

" Beauty is its own excuse for being."

Beauty is thus an end in itself, and has something of the perfection of the completed universe. So far as an object is considered simply as an instrument, so far it ceases to be regarded as beautiful; except, indeed, in cases where it may be regarded as an element in some more comprehensive beauty to which it contributes. The steam-engine as it rushes along its narrow path may

[1] I should consider this aspect of the theme at greater length, if I had not presented it more fully in my *Science of Thought*, under the heading, " Propositions in regard to Beauty."

sometimes seem to us, in its strength and its swift-
ness an object of beauty ; but when this is so we
see it in itself, as the embodiment of a mighty
force.   We do not regard it as a useful machine.

We thus find in beauty a certain unsubstantial-
ity.   What we recognize as characterizing most
especially the material world is the relationship of
action and reaction by which all things are bound
together.   We see working from behind the principle of efficient causation.   On the other side
we recognize that of the final cause.   The first
relation, that of efficient causality, gives us the
world of physical science ; the other, that of the
end or purpose, gives us the world of life, or from
a higher point of view the world of philosophy
and of theology.   Beauty, as such, is taken out
from all these relationships.   Hence that unsubstantial aspect of it which was just named.   We
might picture it, though not with perfect accuracy,
as hovering over the world like a certain divine
image or effluence.   Thus Emerson apostrophizes
it : —

> "Thee gliding through the sea of form
> Like the lightning through the storm,
> Somewhat not to be possessed,
> Somewhat not to be caressed,

No feet so fleet could ever find,
No perfect form could ever bind.
Thou eternal fugitive,
Hovering over all that live."

After having thus considered beauty in general, we have to consider art as a special form of beauty. In entering upon this discussion we must first distinguish between the forms of art that are representative and those that are simply presentative. Among the former the arts of painting and sculpture are the most prominent; among the latter we may reckon architecture and music. Architecture is representative only in certain details. Music very rarely becomes representative or imitative.

The creations of painting and sculpture stand over against the world of nature which they with greater or less accuracy represent. The productions of music and architecture take their place among the works of nature. The former imply thus a certain duality, the image standing apart from the reality. The latter possess a simplicity like that of the music of the winds and the magnificence of the mountains. It is of representative art alone that we have here to speak.

In the whole discussion, it is perhaps needless

to say we must distinguish between the work of art as a thing that has a market value, which thus can be coveted and which may stir the pride of possession, and the work of art as such in its representative character.   In the first aspect it is a thing like other things, and one may stand to it in a personal or private relation.   This is, however, obviously not its nature so far as its artistic character is concerned; so far, that is, as it is representative.   In its primary relation to the spectator, the work of art and the spectator himself stand face to face in the pure world of contemplation ; the world from which all selfish considerations and impulses are removed.

We must notice, also, that representative art has certain subordinate and accidental functions which must be left out of the account in any absolute estimate.   I refer to them simply because some would find in them the distinctive nature of art as contrasted with nature.   By one class of these subordinate functions art works in the line of nature, accomplishing results of the same kind that we find in nature, only accomplishing these more perfectly.   Thus, as we have seen, beauty demands a certain unity and isolation. The beautiful object must seem to be in a manner complete in itself. In nature this result is not always or easily reached. In the landscape, for instance, the various parts or elements are confusedly connected together, and the groupings run into one another. The art of the painter can isolate a single group and present it by itself. It can do more than this. It can bring together elements that in nature are most often scattered, and arrange them with reference to picturesque effect. Thus art can in many cases create a perfection which is rarely found in nature. The painter may select that which is most beautiful in different forms, and unite them in a single ideal form. The creation of the sculptor stands unmarred by the imperfections which are rarely absent in actual life. All of these facts do not, however, mark out a distinct realm for art. The results which have been described are sometimes reached by nature itself. There are landscapes that round themselves into a beautiful completeness which the artist might copy, but which he could not hope to surpass. There are human forms which demand no composition or replacement by elements from other forms, which themselves may stand to the artist as his single and perfect model. If the functions that we have

considered were the only offices of art, art would
be, in a certain sense, the handmaid of nature,
completing that which nature had left imperfect
and perpetuating that which nature had happily
accomplished. All this, however, does not explain the special charm which a pictured landscape, for instance, has as compared with a real
landscape. I do not mean that the charm of the
picture is greater than that of the real landscape.
It may be less; I merely state the commonplace
fact that it is different.

Another subordinate element of power that is
possessed by the artistic representation is that it
enables us to see as if with the eyes of the artist,
so that the scene has something of the glamour
for us that it had for him. This is an element
that must not be spoken lightly of. It is a charm
of which we have all felt the power. Even the
most poetic and sensitive of artists derives, however, from the painting a pleasure different from
that which the landscape itself gives. The power
that comes from the artist's personality is then,
in a sense, accidental. It does not concern the
nature of the painting as such.

It is still less an explanation of our enjoyment
of the painting to ascribe it to our admiration of

the skill of the artist. This would be to degrade art to the level of any work of mere sleight of hand. The recognition of artistic skill may indeed form a subordinate element of our enjoyment of any work of genius ; but this position of subordination must be always kept. So soon as technical skill impresses us more than the real beauty of any artistic creation, the legitimate effect of this, as an object of beauty, is to a very large extent, if not wholly, lost.

We return again, therefore, to the question as to the nature of the special charm which a work of representative art has for us. Since this charm must spring from the peculiar nature of the work it is obvious that its source must be found in its representative character. The work has its peculiar fascination because it is a representation and not a reality. A little thought will show the reasonableness of this position. We have seen that beauty as such is purely an affair of contemplation. We have seen that the beautiful object is thus taken out from the great succession of causation, efficient and final. So far as the spectator enjoys beauty purely as such, so far is he taken out from the realm of strife, longing, and regret. He stands as a mere beholder

absorbed in the joy of contemplation. Now,
that which in the world of realities is accomplished by the power of beauty on the one side,
and the power of abstraction on the other, is, in
the forms of art which we are considering,
accomplished by the artist. The form is separated from the substance. That ethereal beauty
which seemed to float about the reality like a
halo is taken by itself and placed before the eyes
of the beholder. He sees the beauty, and he
sees that this is all. There is no sense of personal relationship. There is no place for fear, or
hope, or longing, in regard to the matters which
are thus presented to him. Thus the perception
of beauty as such, apart from all personal considerations, is made easy, and, if the spectator
have any sense of beauty, is made inevitable.

An illustration of this is found in the fact that
on going out of a picture-gallery the world about
us seems for a few moments to have lost its reality. The distant landscape, the scenes on the
street, the interiors of which we may catch
glimpses, all put themselves into the picturesque
attitude ; we spontaneously strip off the seeming
from the fact, and, accepting this alone, move in
a world of appearances merely.

It may be urged, indeed, that this, also, is no ultimate distinction. The artist and the poet, all who have the sense of beauty, spontaneously assume in the presence of the beauty of nature the attitude of pure contemplation, and thus do not need the help of art in order to accomplish this. This is certainly true. The difference is, however, that while in the enjoyment of natural beauty we may for a moment lose the sense of reality, in the presence of art we have the sense of unreality. That ethereal element which we have found to be one of the properties of beauty is thus forced upon us as it cannot be in the presence of the real objects of nature.

From these general considerations we can understand, in part, the complemental character of painting and sculpture. Each gives only a single aspect of the object represented, thus making obvious and unmistakable the shadowy and unreal character of the presentation. Sculpture gives us the solidity of form without color. Painting gives us color without the solidity of form. There is no possibility of mistaking representation for substitution. That is a cheap triumph of painting that arises from a mistaking the picture for a reality. It is the painting considered as painting which gives us the special pleasure which we derive from it. What is true of painting and sculpture is true, in one sense or another, of all the representative arts. Their function is fulfilled by means of their openly recognized representative character. Thus the drama or the novel differs from history. We may, indeed, study the course of history as if it were a drama or a novel ; but so far as we do this it has ceased to be regarded by us as history. I sat once behind two young girls in the theatre where Ristori represented the sorrows of Marie Antoinette. They gave themselves up to tears of sympathy. Then one would remark, " It is not real; it is only a play," and they would listen for a moment in composure. Then the other would exclaim, " But it is all true, though ; it all happened ! " and then they would surrender themselves anew to their sorrow. It was the struggle between the sense of art and that of reality, even under the circumstances where the art was unmistakable. But even in such an affecting drama as this we see something of the triumph of art. No one of us could bear to look upon the real sorrows of the unhappy queen. The spectacle of the drama moves us, but not to the depths of our heart. The illusion is never so strong that we quite forget that it is an illusion. If we should for a moment really forget that what we see is an illusion, we should not sit as quiet spectators of plots or crime. The rustic at the theatre sometimes cries out, to give warning of some premeditated villainy. Don Quixote at the puppet-show forgot that what he saw was an illusion, and he struck in with his good sword to defend the innocent. Such Don Quixotes should we all become, I trust, if the mimic scene should for a moment be accepted by us as real.

In this recognition of the representative character of art is found the source of at least a part of the pleasure which we derive from it. Even our sorrow is not real sorrow. We are playing at grief, as the actor is playing upon the stage. Doubtless our pleasure is, in part, found in the fact that we can make a playmate of that terrible force of suffering from which at other times we shrink. Now its fierceness is for the moment gone. It is like a wild beast tamed whom we only play that we fear.

It is this representative character which makes possible to art the realism that embraces much

which would otherwise be excluded from its
domain. The beauty of the human form stands
before us in the chaste coldness of the marble ;
and scenes of struggle and suffering that would
in themselves cause us only anguish may serve
to awaken a lofty gladness, as we see imaged before us the triumph of the spirit which finds in
struggle and suffering only the occasion of a
mighty heroism.

We have before seen that one source of our
enjoyment of the beauty of nature is found in the
fact that through it is manifested the presence of
the universal life. The art of which we have been
speaking is to a great extent dead. We have the
lifeless marble and canvas. We have here something quite unlike that life which reveals itself
in plant and animal and man, and in the wide
expanse of nature. If art is representative, it
should represent this also. This absolute life,
it is obvious, admits of no imitation. All that
art can do in the matter is to avoid the semblance
of death. This is accomplished in the arts of
sculpture and painting by that complemental
relation of which I have just spoken. Each of
these gives us only the half of the reality. The
statue is wholly undetermined in the direction of

color. The painting is wholly unreal so far as
the solidity of form is concerned. Each is thus,
in a sense, open to the infinite. We have not
the presence of life, but we do have the absence
of any sense of lifelessness. The bit of colored
wax-work, which for a moment may deceive us
as if by the presence of life, gives us, after the
first glance, the sense of lifelessness. It gives
us the sense of oppression, or else it seems to us
a mere toy. The grandeur of real art comes
from that incompleteness which we have just
considered.

It is a very superficial view that would explain
the pleasure which we derive from the incompleteness of painting and sculpture by the assumption that thereby the imagination of the
beholder is stimulated to complete the work, to
round out the picture, and to color the marble.
This seems to me wholly wrong. Who colors
the marble of the statue in his thought? This
would be to make it imitate the lifeless wax-work ;
or it would be to substitute for it the living form,
and thus to insult its sublime chastity. The
whiteness of the marble, I repeat, produces two
effects. It removes at once the appearance of

life and that of lifelessness. It introduces us into a world with which life and lifelessness have nothing to do, — the world of form. What is true of the statue is true, with the needful qualifications, of the painting.

WE have thus reached certain principles that we must now apply to poetry, which is our special theme. We have found that beauty is, as to its content, the ideal ; as to its form, it is a matter of contemplation only. Of representative art, we have found that its special charm lies in its representative character. The principles which pertain to beauty in general we can apply to our study of poetry without hesitation, for they imply no division in the realm of beauty. So far as poetry is considered as a branch of art, the case is different. There are, as we have seen, two sorts of art, — the representative and the presentative. We have yet to decide whether poetry belongs with painting and sculpture, among the representative arts, or with music and architecture, among the simple, non-representative arts.

As painting is the art that uses color, as sculpture is that which uses marble or some other solid material, and music that which uses sound, so poetry is the art that uses words. As all art must be beautiful from without inwards, or from below upwards, that is, as each artistic work must be beautiful even to the most superficial and uncomprehending glance, and must gain new beauty as we reach more and more to its inmost heart, — the painting, for instance, being beautiful as color, and yet more beautiful in that which the color represents, — so poetry must please even the ear that does not comprehend its real significance. The sounds must form of themselves, to a certain extent, a musical succession. The ear must be charmed also by the regular cadence of the rhythm, and, it may be, pleased with the recurrence of the resembling sounds that mark the rhyme.

Besides this pleasure which the ear derives from rhyme and rhythm, the nature of which pleasure I will not here further discuss, these characteristics of poetry add still further to its charm. In the first place, they aid in constructing that unity which every object of beauty needs. Each line and each stanza is by its completed measure formed into a whole; and these separate wholes, united, form the grand whole, which is the poem. The poem is thus shut off from all entanglement with the activities and utilities of life. It stands as a simple and single object of contemplation.

One very important result of the unity thus reached is found in the fact that each part contains in itself a power that comes from the whole. The whole is, in a sense, present in every part. We know how the movement of some vast and orderly proeession expresses the feeling of joy or sorrow more than a moving, unorganized mass of people. Especially is this the case when the music, to the rhythm of which all move, seems to utter the emotion common to all. Every individual seems to represent the whole. So the organizing power that manifests itself in the poem seems to concentrate itself at every point at once; and words and phrases express vastly more, and have a far greater force and beauty, than they would have had in prose. Even a quotation torn from its surroundings, yet bearing with it the movement of the rhythm which belonged to the whole, retains something of this added power.

Another result of the rhythmical form is that words are to some extent freed from that bondage to mere use which is so largely felt in prose. The most effective words and the most effective arrangement of words may be chosen. Words and arrangements of words that would sound affected in prose do not sound affected in poetry, because poetry belongs to the world of beauty and not to that of use. It is as in the pomp of a procession, in which trappings and uniforms may be worn that would be absurd in the office or counting-room ; and a regular and stately stride can be maintained which would be ridiculous if one were simply going to his place of business.

Further, rhythm and rhyme accomplish for the creations of the poetic art what is accomplished for the creations of painting and sculpture by the material which they employ. They show that what is placed before us is not the reality, but the appearance. Men sometimes ridicule the conversations which in the opera are carried on in song, and in the drama in verse. They might as well insist on the absurdity of the whiteness of a marble statue. Each art uses its own material, and thereby shows that it is an art. The thin classicalities of an earlier poetry contributed to the same effect of unreality. They showed the utterance of the poem to be in some

way foreign to the realities of life. They proved
to be, however, too great a refinement. The
measure itself is sufficient for this end, and all
else tends to make the representation seem vacant.
Rhythm and rhyme accomplish this severance
from the world of actuality by means of art ; the
classicalities just referred to did this artificially.
Rhyme and rhythm do this, because they form
the material with which poetry works, as painting
works with color, and sculpture with form. Together they make up the most melodious speech.
The classicalities did this by adding something
foreign and needless.

Goethe recognizes in a striking manner the
effect of rhyme and rhythm in giving a certain
air of unreality to the scenes depicted, when, in a
letter to Schiller, he speaks of transforming the
closing scene of the first part of the "Faust"
from prose to poetry. He says in effect that
when rhyme is used, the meaning is seen through
it as through a veil, and the direct working of the
terrible scene is softened.

The question that we left unanswered is thus
settled for us. Poetry must be reckoned among
the representative arts. Even in its lyrical form,
it does not directly express passion ; it represents

passion. It is the picture, not the reality. A
man under the pressure, let us say, of some
great grief, would hardly find the direct and
natural expression of his sorrow in the artificial
methods of poetry. A rhythmic utterance passion may, indeed, naturally assume; but the
measuring of lines, the search for rhymes, the
testing the musical effect of consonants and vow-
els as they succeed one another, all this is not
the natural utterance of sorrow. What is true of
sorrow is true of the other passions. From our
study of other representative arts, we should
expect to find poetry dealing with representations, not with realities; the form of poetry shows
this to be the case. We must, then, insist that
poetry is a representative art.

Although the result just stated seems to have
been proved, it may appear to us hardly in accordance with the truth. We feel that the poem
deals with realities. The conceits of Cowley we
call artificial because they are the products of art
rather than nature. Thus, wherever we find
marks of excessive art, we deny that the poetry is
real poetry. This would seem to imply that true
poetry is not art but nature. Poetry has to do
with reality because it represents reality. We

have here the most wonderful exhibition of the
power of self-consciousness. The passion must
be there. The poet must feel; yet he must in
some sense put the feeling outside of himself, —
must, as one has said, hold it at arm's length and
contemplate it, and then he must copy it in his
verse. The poem is representative, but the reality must be there in order that it may be represented.

Perhaps this mingling of the reality and the
semblance may be best expressed by the statement that the feeling as uttered in the poem is no
longer individual; it has become universal. We
have seen that all art deals with the typical; in
other words with the ideal. It is so with poetry.
It utters the private joys or loves or sorrows of a
single heart in such a way that the utterance
may stand for the joys, the loves, and the sorrows of all hearts. The poet's private possession
of his own mood is lost. His individual emotion
is swallowed up in the universal expression.
Thus his own mood hovers before him as a matter of contemplation, as something that belongs
to the race rather than to himself. It is accepted by the race as belonging to it rather than
to him.

We thus understand the relief that poetry brings to the overcharged heart. The cry relieves by setting free the pent-up energies of the nature. The poem relieves by taking the emotion for the moment out from the heart that felt it, placing it over against the spirit so that it looks upon it as if from the outside. This may be illustrated by some of the most famous poems of sorrow. Milton and Shelley placed at the head of their utterances of grief, not the names of the friends for whom they sorrowed, but strange names, — Lycidas and Adonais. It was as much as to say, It is not our sorrow that we utter: it is the world's sorrow. Emerson expresses something the same feeling with a sublime *naïveté* in his " Threnody " : —

> " Not mine ; I never called thee mine,
> But Nature's heir."

We have thus reached the reconciliation of the two definitions of poetry with which we started. We have found that poetry is an imitative art ; we have found also the necessity of passion in poetry. Though the passion be not directly uttered, yet its presence is implied. If poetry is representative, there must be some reality that is represented. We criticise the conceits of Cowley, for instance, not because they are in the strictest sense of the term artificial, but because they are poor art. They do not really represent that which they profess to represent. There is, indeed, one passion of which poetry is the more direct expression than of any other. It is the passion for which an indirect expression may be the most natural and real. It is the passion for the ideal itself. It is any form of real admiration, love, or reverence. The worshipper elaborates the temple, or works out the image, of his divinity with tender care, because by such care alone can he show his reverence. The painter who is a lover of nature works with a like tenderness and a like care, as he strives to represent those traits which are so precious to him; and this very care, this very delicacy of treatment, testifies to the love with which he works. This passion for the ideal must underlie all art, and therefore all poetry. This passion need not express itself by adjectives of emotion, though these may have their place. Its truest expression is the fidelity and the typical truth of the picture itself. Look, for instance, at the power of the poem, "Dies Iræ." The translator speaks of "that awful day." The original hardly needs to tell us that the day is an awful one.

To say that poetry is not the direct expression of passion, but that it presents its image only, may seem at first sight to make a distinction where there is very little difference. The distinction, however, is one of fundamental importance. It solves many of the difficulties that have beset the theory of poetry, and answers many of the questions that have arisen in regard to it. Before applying the principle to such solution of problems, we must first be sure that the distinction itself is perfectly clear to our minds.

The expression of passion is natural, spontaneous, and in extreme cases irrepressible. Such expression may take form in complaint, in invective, in praise, or in exultation. A perception of the artificial, of the manufactured, in such expression, weakens it and makes it unreal. On the other hand, the image or representation of passion is a product of conscious art. In it we demand, indeed, the very perfection of art. For such representation poetry is, for the reasons that have been given, especially fitted, though of course prose may be used for the same purpose.

Again, the expression of passion, so far as it

has a conscious end, is meant to draw attention to one's self. It is meant, perhaps, to secure help; at least it is meant to win sympathy. This is not an unworthy motive. The stricken heart longs for sympathy and is comforted by it. On the other hand, the representation of the passion has no such individual aim. Its object is not to win sympathy, but to create an object of beauty. If any personal aim is mingled with this, it is the hope for fame. In his loftiest mood, the poet hopes to add to the treasures of the world another thing of beauty that shall be to it "a joy forever," — a joy even though the beauty that it presents be the beauty of sorrow. Who, for instance, thinks of Tennyson in reading the " In Memoriam," except so far as one thinks of him to admire and wonder at his genius? Who, in reading the "In Memoriam," pities Tennyson for the loss of such a friend as he describes? Who dreams that Tennyson wrote to win such sympathy? As we read, we are entranced by the beauty of sorrow as it is imaged in melodious verse. We rejoice still more in the beauty of a faith that conquers sorrow. If from this admiration we pass by reflection to the thought of the reality that underlies the whole, we reach, not

the individual, but the universal. We feel, in
the familiar language of the poem itself, that

> " 'Tis better to have loved and lost
> Than never to have loved at all."

It is this we feel, not the special sorrow of the
individual who wrote the poem.

The fact that poetry is a representative art,
and the difference between representation and
direct expression, may now be assumed to be
clear. It remains to apply the result that we
have reached to the explanation of certain characteristics of poetry.

Dr. Holmes, in his work on Emerson, illustrates by a witty conceit . the fact, that confi-
dences which in prose would seem too personal
for utterance are accepted in poetry as in perfect taste. The true explanation of this fact is
found in the principle which we have just
reached. In the poem we have the image, not
the reality. In reading the poem we do not
think of the individuality of the author, but simply of the song he sings; or, if we think of him,
it is only to thank him for the song.

The principle that we have established enables us to understand why some persons have
no taste for poetry. They have what we call

prosaic souls. While poetry has to do with the image, they are bound to the real ; while poetry has to do with the universal, they cannot escape from the power of the individual. They either see no worth in the mere formal representation, or they at once pass through it to the special fact which it represents. It has been said of such that they have no imagination. I am not quite sure of this. They imagine the scene so distinctly that it seems to them real. The difficulty is that they cannot rest in the world of the imagination, but rush through to the fact behind.

The general results that have been reached enable us to explain why certain themes are not suitable for poetry.

Since poetry is the representation and not the expression of passion, certain feelings are obviously unfitted for its use, namely, those that are so intense that the poet cannot separate himself from them, cannot hold himself aloof to draw their image. Such is the sorrow that is most strong in contrast with

" The lesser griefs that may be said."

Since poetry, like all art and all beauty, is something for contemplation alone, we find a further limitation of the field of poetry, and indeed of all art, in the fact that nothing can be fitly imaged which is of such a nature that the spectator, the reader, or the hearer cannot rest with the image. This is the case if the image tends to excite longing or disgust or horror, as if the real object were present. The line here indicated may be, indeed, somewhat conventional. In the classic days of the French drama, effects were excluded which we now contemplate with equanimity ; but still there is a point at which the line is real and not conventional.

A further limitation of the material which is suitable for poetry is found in the fact that, like all art and all beauty, it is the manifestation of the ideal.

There has been much discussion as to the relative claims of idealism and realism. The discussion has been sometimes confused by the fact that the difference between idealism and realism has not been clearly, or at least not truly, discerned. The ideal, as we have already seen, properly implies the typical or characteristic. Beauty is the manifestation of the ideal ; representative art is the representation of this. The qualifications which these statements require have been glanced at in the earlier part of this discussion. In this use of the term, which I conceive is the only proper one, the "idealist," in the truest sense of the word, is the "realist" as well. We may thus understand the fallacy of that so-called realism which assumes that one aspect of life, if it be only actual, is as fit a subject for painting or poetry as any other. Man is an animal, but his animality is not that which is most distinctive of him as a man, and therefore is not the true matter for poetry. That is a true idealism which demands in poetry some hint at least of the ideal or typical man. This does not mean that poetry must always assume the *grande manière*, or that only the angelic is a fit theme for song. Man is not an angel, and the angelic is, therefore, not that which is most typical of him; and naturalness, above all things, is to be demanded. Even the lower aspects of life, up to a certain limit, may be exhibited, if they are illuminated by something higher than themselves; or if they set off the higher by contrast, as in that line of Tennyson, terribly realistic in the lower sense of the word : —

" Feeding like horses when you hear them feed."

The same may be done in satire and invective, where, however, we pass out from the realm of

poetry as, in the strict sense of the word, a fine
art.

We may notice here a curious distinction.
Even the temperance man may sing drinking
songs, but the glutton does not sing eating songs.
We can sing : —

> " O landlord fill the flowing bowl !"

We cannot sing : —

> O landlord bring the loaded platter !

There is a god of the wine-cup.   I know of no
god of the tureen.   Bacchus, the god of the vine,
came drinking.   Ceres, the goddess of grain, did
not come eating.   The difference is that, while
eating belongs to the essential necessities of our
individual lives, the cup kindles the imagination.
It tends, for the moment, to free one from the
prosaic details of life.   It brings a semblance,
poor, tawdry, disappointing, and hindering indeed,
but yet a semblance, of the higher and freer life
of the spirit.

We understand by the principle that has been
developed why a mere list of objects, such as
Walt Whitman sometimes gives, is not poetry.
We see where poetry begins.   Poetry, like all
representative art, begins with the construction

of an image; and a name is not an image.
Poetry involves a certain idealizing element;
that is, the image of a beautiful object should
bring out the special traits that make the thing ·
what it is. We call it a low stage of art where
the boy has to write beneath his picture, " This
is a horse." But suppose the words to be written
without the image. In this case we have neither
art nor poetry. In poems such as have been referred to we have the " This is a horse " without the picture. Walt Whitman, however, gives
us not merely lists. He gives us pictures also,
more or less complete. These are crowded together, some repulsive, some terrible, some beautiful. They are like faces that peer at us for a
moment in a dream. They are like forms that
are swept past by some rushing river, — that
emerge for a moment and then sink back into the
swirl. But poetry, like all art, demands a certain
completeness. In Italy one sometimes sees a
wall in which bits of sculpture and bas-relief are
mingled with common stones. Such a wall is
interesting, but it is not art. I am happy to add
that now and then Walt Whitman manifests his
strength without the extravagance into which
false theories of art have led him.

If our principle shows us where poetry begins, it also shows us where it ends. Poetry is a representative art. It is a process of imaging in words. Even though the image be so tenuous that it cannot be reduced to the terms of the senses, it must nevertheless exist. There must be a vision, an *anschauung*, though it be for the subtilest perception of the spirit alone. There must be a fusing of elements into a unity in which they exist only as the parts of an undivided and indivisible whole. No mere intellectual statement, no mathematical or philosophical problem, can be poetry, because there is no such image on the one side, and no such vision on the other. The imagination had nothing to do with its creation, and to the imagination it does not appeal. This fact is what, as I suppose, Milton had in mind when he said that poetry should be sensuous. At any rate, it expresses whatever truth there is in this statement.

A prominent metaphysician quotes four lines from what he calls a beautiful poem. The lines are these : —

> " The essence of mind's being is the stream of thought,
>   Difference of mind's being is difference of the stream ;
> Within this single difference may be brought
>   The countless differences that are or seem."

The poem as a whole may be beautiful, but these lines are certainly not poetry. But why, it may be asked, are they not poetry? There is certainly an image, and the image is not one of mere comparison; it is a metaphor, in which the elements that are compared are fused together. The mind is called a stream. The answer is that the figure is conventional and merely explanatory. There is no construction by the imagination. It is, further, abstract. We neither see by the imagination, nor conjecture by the intellect, what are the " differences of the stream " referred to. Is it that the stream moves more or less rapidly? That it is more or less turbid? That it is broader or narrower? There was no stream present to the mind of the writer. The figure is merely what a familiar phrase would call, by an unintended satire, " a figure of speech."

From all that has been said, we may see something of the sweep of poetry.. It may represent whatever stirs the heart to admiration. It may image all emotion or passion that contains the beginning of a larger life, that takes one in any sense out of one's self; or it may rise to the loftiest heights which imagination can reach, checked only by the thin air in which its wings

arc powerless. It may represent the passion of
the lover, who finds his ideal embodied in a human form; or it may sing with Wordsworth the
not less passionate love of nature; or like Emerson, with equal passion, it may hymn the praise
of the absolute ideal of beauty which manifests
itself in all fair forms of nature and life : —

> " All that's good and great with thee
> Works in close conspiracy ;
> Thou hast bribed the dark and lonely
> To report thy features only,
> And the cold and purple morning,
> Itself with thoughts of thee adorning."

Or, if only the form be that of vision rather
than mere intellectual utterance, it may hymn
the praise of that infinite Presence which is the
creator and the inspiration of beauty, — a height
of song which Wordsworth and Emerson have
reached in their loftiest flights.

This passion for the ideal is not, as some have
thought, an intellectual appreciation. It is the
rapture of the heart, and not merely a recognition of the thought.

We cannot leave our theme without adding a
word in regard to the ethical aspect of poetry.
In itself, poetry has no moral character. What

is called "didactic poetry" is poetry only as to its form. Precepts of morality are not poetry, any more than propositions of geometry or philosophy. It is true, indeed, that moral truth may be fused by the imagination, and cast into such a form of beauty that the result is a work of art, independently of the lesson that one would teach. This is simply to say that moral facts, like so many other facts, may be treated æsthetically. Take, as a magnificent example, Tennyson's "Palace of Art." Here we have the tragedy of a soul

"That did love Beauty only ;
. . . . . . seeing not
That Beauty, Good, and Knowledge are three sisters
That never can be sundered without tears."

The tragedy is a real one ; as real as that of Clytemnestra, and more terrible than that. The one, as truly as the other, presented itself to the poet in its æsthetic aspect, and is so accepted by the reader ; and we may draw a lesson as truly from the one as from the other.

We must notice, in passing, that the lines quoted from Tennyson do not touch the question as to whether art should have an end beyond itself. The soul was guilty because it "did love beauty only." It would live in a palace of art from which all the realities of life were excluded. It does not follow that its art should have had an ethical aim, but simply that the soul itself should have had an ethical aim. We are taught that the world of art does not furnish the complete environment of the spirit.   ·

So far as the battle between the defender of "art for art's sake," on the one side, and the moralist on the other, is concerned, I hold that the former is right in his principle, while the latter is right in certain of his results. Some of the material which the moralist would exclude from art on moral grounds, I would exclude on artistic grounds. In discussing the matter of realism and idealism, we saw that there is a line, vague and uncertain indeed, yet real, beyond which material suited for æsthetic representation cannot be sought. This outlying material should be excluded from art for the sake of art itself.

It is true that "to the pure all things are pure." This is because the pure mind is content to accept the reserves of nature. In violating these, the art that prides itself upon its natural-ness has become unnatural, and is, so far, false art. To the clean all things are clean ; but that is because the cleanly person is not fond of dabbling in the dirt. He knows how to keep the proper relations of things, and only for that reason is he clean. No more than another could he touch pitch without being defiled.

On the other hand, it must be admitted that poetry, like all art, may be harmful to the best life. As Tennyson's poem has just shown us, art may harm the spirit by detaching it from all earnest purpose, and placing it in a world of contemplation alone. All æsthetic pleasure, the love of nature itself, may accomplish the same result. Further, poetry may, by the halo that it casts about them, allure the spirit to lower joys, even without crossing the line at which art ceases to be art. — Naturally, however, poetry works for good. It may detach the spirit from bondage to the petty, hard, and often debasing facts of life. It may take something of their grossness from the lowest joys ; while the spirit that will yield itself to its guidance may be led by it towards the contemplation of that highest ideal which is the one absolute reality.

THE POETIC ASPECT OF NATURE.

THE material with which poetry has to do may be regarded under two general divisions. One of these is the world of nature; the other is that of human life. The former I consider under the present heading. One important aspect of the latter will be discussed in the next chapter.

In the study of "The Philosophy of Poetry," we glanced at the conditions under which the external world becomes beautiful to us; and recognized the relation of man to nature, out from which the enjoyment of natural beauty springs. All this, however, even if we were able to study it more profoundly, would not justify the peculiar charm which nature has for us, — the charm which has inspired some of the loftiest poetry, and which is felt by all who have any touch of the poetic inspiration. Indeed, there is prevalent a view of the world, that is not wholly without foundation, which would seem to make this delight in nature impossible.

There is perhaps no contrast in literature more striking than that between the essay of John Stuart Mill, entitled "Nature," and the essay of Emerson which bears the same name. Both would picture to us the same reality. In the one case, however, we find ourselves in the presence of a demon; in the other, of a divinity. There may be some exaggeration in both these representations. Certainly Mill fails to recognize some elements of the theme. "In sober truth," he tells us, "nearly all the things which men are hanged or imprisoned for doing to each other are nature's every-day performances;" and here follows a picture of the suffering and death which nature is constantly producing. Pope's

"Shall gravitation cease when you go by"

is quoted with derision. "A man who should persist in hurling stones or firing cannon when another man 'goes by,' and having killed him urge a similar plea in extenuation, would very deservedly be found guilty of murder."—This of course depends upon circumstances. It is not so in war, for instance. There may be occupations in which the stones or the cannon-balls might not be kept back even for a friend who might be in the way, as the lightening of a suddenly sink-

ing ship, or the defence of a hardly pressed fort,
where a moment's delay might make the difference between common loss and safety. The
execution of the public laws cannot turn out of
its way for individuals. If we consider that the
stability of the universe depends upon the stead-
fastness of the laws of nature, the criticism of
Mill will seem trivial.

Whether in the statements of Emerson there
be or be not any similar exaggeration, is a matter of mood and sentiment. The merely prosaic
mind may perhaps fail to enter into the fulness
of his enthusiasm. But a mood and a sentiment are to a great extent their own justification.
They prove at least the adequateness of their
cause. In the lives of many, indeed, there are
times when the words of Emerson would seem
to be so true as to be commonplace. They express the poetic view of nature. The poets
abound in similar utterances. Much of our modern poetry is based upon a similar conception ;
we enjoy the expression of it and do not doubt
its truth. The words of Emerson are, however,
so clear and so felicitous that, perhaps better
than any others, they may be contrasted with the
utterance of Mill, and all the more pointedly

since they express the poetic sentiment in plain prose.

The curious contrast between these essays is heightened by the fact that both contain so much truth. That of Mill, in spite of some exaggeration, presents an aspect of nature that cannot be overlooked. The forces of nature certainly have no respect for persons. In this sense nature may not be called immoral, but she is certainly unmoral. Through all the ranks of the lower nature there prevails, to a large extent, a commonplace selfishness. I call it selfishness because each plant and animal is pressing to maintain itself, to satisfy its own needs and desires, with little thought, for the most part, for others. I call this selfishness commonplace, because it concerns simply the most ordinary wants of life. The satisfaction of these wants is elevated by no lofty sentiments or ideas. An elephant, for instance, is a beast that by its vastness, its gentleness, its gravity, its intelligence, has an air of nobility. I confess there is something about it almost akin to sublimity. On the other hand there is something humiliating, almost painful, in seeing this magnificent beast begging for gingerbread or peanuts, there is such intentness, such absorption in the plea. So, too, a horse is full of spirit and life. There seems something akin to genius about him. His rider cannot help imagining him as the companion of his loftiest sentiments, if not of his loftiest thoughts. But how the hope of a bit of sugar or an apple will absorb the whole nature of the horse! How eager he is, and when the demand is gratified, what delight! These examples are types of the life of the lower world. We speak of nature as one; but nature is an accumulation of petty lives, each absorbed in the pursuit of the lowest ends. The voices of the woods which thrill our hearts, the form of bird or beast or reptile which steals across our view, the stateliness of the tree, the beauty of the flower, all are examples of the same kind of life; all bear signs of the warfare or the victory in this strife for the lowest ends.

Science, at first exalting us by its revelations, in the end makes the universe more prosaic than it was before. What visions we had of the life among the stars! What lofty societies of spirits purer and wiser than ours did we imagine to be holding blissful intercourse on some distant orb, or even on our own magnificent sun! But

science has kindled fires that have burned up
our fair imaginings. What habitable systems
may be lurking around these grander bodies we
cannot say ; but certainly these blazing worlds do
not offer themselves as homes for any kind of
population with which we would care to people
them. Within our own day a book has been
published containing, among other things, argu-
ments to prove that the sun is the abode of glorified spirits. We now know that if any spirits
dwell among its raging flames they cannot be the
glorified. Even the color and fragrance of the
flower, science puts into her most prosaic categories. They are simply the means by which
certain classes or species have preserved their
being by making themselves conspicuous enough
to attract the fertilizing bee.

We thus grant the essential truthfulness of
Mill's picture of nature. Taken in detail, nature
is commonplace and selfish. Taken as a whole,
it is heartless and indifferent. In the great
struggle for existence, it is an impartial and un-
interested umpire. Whether it be the serpent or
the dove, whether it be the devil-fish or man, its
judgment is that the victor shall survive and the
vanquished perish. What place is then left for

the fine enthusiasm of Emerson ? What is there in this nature to so touch and exalt the heart ?

While we ask the question, even before we ask the question, we feel that he also is right. Even while we uttered what seemed to be the hard, commonplace facts in regard to nature, the very forms of which we spoke made us feel, in the very naming of them, the power of their beauty. We pictured the stars as they really are, merely vast fire-balls; but while we spoke, the very thought of them awed us by the memory of their lofty presence. We showed the commonplace origin of the scent and color of the flowers ; and while we spoke of them, the memory of their beauty found its way into our hearts. So the lover tries to chide his mistress for some fault, but while he speaks her beauty smiles away his wrath, and the words begun in anger end in love.

The fascination and the exalting power of nature remain, then, real, in spite of all the ugly and prosaic facts which we can accumulate. John Stuart Mill, whose harsh criticism of nature formed our starting-point, may himself be a witness to this strange power. At one time in his youth he fell into a deep melancholy which obstructed the exercise of all his powers, taking away his interest in what had been most attractive. The charm that dissipated the cloud which brooded over his life was found in the poems of Wordsworth. His songs soothed the troubled spirit of this leader of men, as the harp of David did that of Saul. But the songs of Wordsworth are simply the breath of nature. In them she finds a voice. The healing power, then, was that of nature of which he afterwards spoke, as we have seen, so rudely. This soothing and recreating power of nature is beautifully painted in the beginning of the second part of the great poem of Goethe. No translation can give any idea of the eloquence and completed beauty of the verse in which is described this baptism into nature of the sin-stained and world-weary Faust.

We may then listen without remonstrance to the words of Emerson when he places nature over against man as his superior. "In the wilderness," he tells us, "I find something more dear and connate than in streets or villages. In the tranquil landscape, and especially in the distant line of the horizon, man beholds something as beautiful as his own nature." And elsewhere

even the "wise men and eminent souls" seem to
him a result unworthy of the nature out from
which they came.   We can find no more striking recognition in poetry of this relation between
man and nature than the following lines from
Keats : —

> "Yes, in spite of all,
> Some shape of beauty moves away the pall ·
> From our dark spirits.   Such the sun, the moon ;
> Trees, old and young, sprouting a shady boon
> For simple sheep ; and such are daffodils,
> With the green world they live in ; and clear rills
> That for themselves a cooling covert make
> 'Gainst the hot season ; the mid-forest brake,
> Rich with a sprinkling of fair musk-rose blooms ;
> And such, too, is the grandeur of the dooms
> We have imagined for the mighty dead."

We read these lines without any feeling save
that of enjoyment of the luxuriant beauty which
they present to us ; but when we fairly think of
them in the light of the contrast we have been
considering, we can but ask what is there in run-
ning water, in trees and flowers, that should
make them worthy to rank as the equals of the
dooms

> "We have imagined for the mighty dead."

This is all true for our feeling ; but from the
point of view of our reflection, the simplest pres-

ence of conscious thought and love and aspiration would seem to be worth infinitely more than
the mechanical movements of unorganized nature,
the dull, uneventful, unconscious life of the plant,
and the merely sensuous existence of bird and
animal. A single true and loving soul would
seem to be a worthy outcome of all the mighty
play of elemental forces from which have issued
the worlds of organized life.

The question then forces itself upon us, What
is the secret of the joy we take in the lower
nature, and of the soothing and uplifting power
which it has for us ?

The fundamental paradox is found in the fact
upon which we have already dwelt, namely, that
on the one side the forms of nature are either
lifeless, or manifest a very low order of vitality ;
that nature herself is unconscious, and unmoral
if not immoral : and on the other side, that this
nature has such power over us, that the most
pressing interests of our human life and our
loftiest spiritual culture should to any seem in-
significant in comparison with it.

The solution of any difficulty is found often
nearest its heart, and perhaps we may in this
case find some hint of the solution where the

antithesis of the elements is most marked. I am not sure that the unmorality of nature which troubles Mr. Mill so much is not one source of its charm. In life we are pressed by two sorts of spectres: those of duties to be done, and those of duties left undone. Or if this statement is too strong, there is at least

> "The yoke of conscience masterful
> That galls us everywhere."

In our intercourse with others, in our observation of the affairs of life, we carry the same standard. All are judged, not merely by their pleasantness, but also by their conformity to the great standard of right.

In the presence of nature we escape this thrall. There in the solitude the claims of the world lose their hold upon us. We are in the presence of a life which is its own law. Self-seeking with it is not meanness, repose is not idleness, play is not frivolousness. There is no time to be improved; therefore there is no time to be wasted. There is nothing to be done; therefore there is nothing left undone. Each individual is a law to itself, and life is only play.

Charles Lamb defended the comedies of a not over-moral age against the charge of immorality.

He maintained that in them we simply enter a realm to which the rules of our morality do not apply. The creations of the comedy are not men and women to be praised or blamed ; and in this fact he found in part the charm of these artistic works. It does not follow from this that Charles Lamb would like to live himself in such a world; that the ethical restraints of society were really irksome to him ; that he would gladly be free to talk and act like the heroes of the play : it means simply that he felt it a pleasure and a diversion to contemplate this free world which was so unlike his own.

Something akin to this may be, in part, the pleasure which we take in the world of nature. Nature is deeper, larger, tenderer than that mimic world ; but still it involves something of the same sense of freedom.

But this is only one aspect of the complete relation of the life of nature to our human life. The restraint of morality is only one example of the limitation by which our human life is bound. Personality, self-consciousness, these in a certain sense mark limits. Self-consciousness shuts off sharply my life from the lives about me. It shuts it off also from the universal life. Everything connected with our human society bears marks of the same limitation. In one aspect of the case, we can say indeed that the products of our human civilization are as natural as the products of vegetable and animal life. A man builds his house by an instinct like that by which the bird builds its nest. Our cities grow where nature placed them. Caprice only now and then interferes with the great laws that guide the choice of a city's site. Our manufacturing establishments are as natural as the beaver's dam; our political institutions as natural as those of the bees and the ants; the course of trade and that of civilization itself are as natural as the courses of the streams. If, then, all the creations of our human life are as natural as the products of the forests, it would appear that we should take the same kind of pleasure in them. The fact, however, is that we do not. The feeling with which we walk the streets of a city, however tasteful and elegant these streets may be, is of a nature utterly unlike that with which we tread the aisles of the forest, or the path which leads up some mountain side. Human works, with certain exceptions to be hereafter named, bear the marks of human limitation. Even the animals that consort with man bear trace of it. A horse, however beautiful, does not affect us like a stag, nor a dog like a squirrel. A cat, perhaps, bears less the mark of this human limitation than other domestic animals. While with us, a cat is rarely of us. She lets herself be fed and petted, but keeps her own counsel, and is in general, in the midst of our civilization, as much a piece of nature as the stream that dashes through our garden.

This limitation is nothing merely accidental and transient. It is to a large extent the very condition of human development. Intelligence is by its very nature discrimination. The understanding, is, as we have seen, the analyzer. The greater the intelligence, the greater the discrimination. An understanding developed to infinity would imply an infinite analysis. By the understanding the man separates his life from the lives about him. He shuts these off sharply from one another. He separates his own ends and aims, and sets each distinctly before himself. Each at the moment excludes the others, just as each life excludes all other lives. Thus the development of the understanding implies an infinite limitation. It implies determination, and "all determination is limitation." Thus every human work is the expression, not merely of a single human life which had, in the manner indicated, consciously shut itself off from all other lives; it is the expression, not of the whole even of this single life, but of a single idea or purpose which was consciously held at the moment, distinct from all others.

Now such absolute limitation is destructive to the highest æsthetic sense, which is primarily a sense of freedom. This may be illustrated by a principle laid down by Ruskin that every interior represented in a picture should have in some way an opening into the infinite.

I have stated that this limitation is true of human works with some exceptions. These exceptions are found in the creations of the highest art. Yet even those do not affect us in the manner in which we are moved by the works of nature. I would not compare the two, for that is not my present theme. I will admit that the inspiration derived from a work of the highest art may be to some minds more intense than that derived from nature, but still the inspiration is of a different quality. In art we rarely escape fully the sense of artificialness. If ever we do wholly escape this in the presence of human art, I think that it is most often in the presence of religious architecture. The kinship between the beauty of nature and that of the ideally perfect temple may be illustrated by the fact that, when the aisle of a forest vaguely suggests that of a church, the æsthetic effect is deepened. This, I think, is not true of any other resemblance between the works of nature and those of man. Other resemblances may interest or amuse us, but they lie out of the range of the æsthetic pleasure.

We have thus far considered our theme merely negatively. We have seen that in the presence of the life of nature we escape the limitation of human life and of human works. This mere negative element is, however, not sufficient. This may be escaped in the sand plain as well as in the forest. There is needed for the full result a positive element. Our enjoyment of nature is not merely an escape ; it is also a meeting : not merely an emptying, but a fulfilling.

In nature we are brought into the presence of a fulness of life. By a fulness of life I mean a life that is not cut up into a multitude of lives, which lives are in turn cut up into a multitude of thoughts and purposes. By life I do not mean merely organized life, the life of plant and animal. In nature itself is a life. We feel the presence of this life in the mountain and the cataract, as truly as in the flower and the bird. In one sense this life of nature has undergone infinite division. Every animal, every plant, every leaf, is distinct from every other. But yet this distinctness is only superficial. The separateness is merely for the beholder, not for the things themselves. They do not discriminate themselves from one another. Conscious separateness does not exist. The unity affects us more than the difference. Hills and rivers, trees and animals, flowers and birds, are separate existences only in the sense in which the different leaves of the same tree are separate existences. They are simply different manifestations of a common life.

What is more, we feel vaguely and indistinctly indeed, but still really, that this life is ours also; that we ourselves are not merely separate individualities, but that we also are manifestations of this common life. Hence comes in part the freedom that we feel in such contemplation. We are called out of ourselves. We forget ourselves.

We live only in the large, unfettered life about us, and that for the moment lives in us.

But difficulties still meet us. After all, this life is lower than ours, or must we admit that consciousness is lower than unconsciousness? This would imply that the great movement of a development that has culminated in man has been a descent, not an elevation. This we cannot admit. We must still insist that the life of nature is inferior to the life of man. So far, then, we have nothing to account for the enjoyment which we take in nature. If we would find a sufficient basis for this, we must seek some other aspects of the case in which this inferiority does not exist.

We find one element of that which we demand in the fact that the life of nature is *the all* of which our individual lives are parts. In nature is the full and as yet undivided life, with the infinite promise of which the most perfect individual lives are only the partial fulfilment. The older poets loved to speak of the earth as our mother. Nature is indeed our mother. All that we have and are we have received from her. Thus we may well turn to her not only with love, but with reverence also.

We have already recognized the fact that the love of nature has reached in these later days a conscious strength of which we find little trace in the classic poets.   That the Greeks and Romans loved nature there can be no doubt.   They recognized her, as we have seen, as their mother. The glimpses of nature that we meet continually in the poems of Homer, for example, show an appreciation of natural beauty.   The peopling of wood and stream with divinities was born out of this love of nature.   We find, even among those most full of the modern feeling towards the outer world some who look back with longing to the conception which the Greeks had of a living nature.   Lotze seeks a view of nature which may supply to us the loss of this elder consciousness.   At the same time it is true that there is a keener and more conscious delight in the beauty of nature as such, in these later days, than, there ever was before.   We must admit that this higher view exists side by side with a low, prosaic, and mechanical view of nature far inferior to that of the ancients.   Wordsworth recognizes the lower view, that is too common in these days of mechanical marvels, in his indignant cry : —

"Great God! I 'd rather be
A pagan suckled in a creed outworn,
So might I, standing on this pleasant lea,
Have glimpses that would make me less forlorn,
Have sight of Proteus rising from the sea,
Or hear old Triton blow his wreathèd horn."

Yet Wordsworth felt, and at other times expressed, a love of nature of which, whether under
the form of the dizzy rapture of youth, or the
calmer though not less intense joy of manhood,
the "pagan" could not have conceived. In ancient
poetry, nature figures chiefly as a background for
human life. The Greeks were so at one with
nature that they could not easily conceive either
of themselves as separate from it or of it as
separate from themselves. Thus the charms of
nature present themselves more often as mingled
with their thoughts and contemplations than as
objects of their thoughts and contemplations.
For this last result, that is, for the full recognition of the life and beauty of nature apart from
any relation to human activity, there was needed
a grand convulsion like that which Christianity
introduced. Christianity exalted the soul, making it the only object of care and interest. The
spiritual life detached itself wholly from the
earthly life. It found in itself infinite possibili-

ties entirely independent of the world. Thus it came to despise the attractions of the earth. It found in nature no loveliness. It rather had of it a dread and horror. This chasm between the spiritual and the natural was the necessary condition of that fuller and freer communion with nature which we now enjoy. When the intensity of that first strain upon the spirit had spent itself, or rather when the spirit had become at last so secure of itself that it no longer needed to maintain its own distinct life by repelling all the elements by which it is surrounded, it began to look about itself, and to make for itself again a home upon the earth. It began to feel itself again at one with nature. But this nature with which it felt itself at one was no longer a mere part of itself. It was its opposite. The two — the soul within and the nature without — still stood over against one another: but the antithesis was no longer one of opposition; it was the necesary condition of the perception of the real beauty and power of nature; the condition of the surrender of itself by the spirit to nature as to some thing at one with yet distinct from itself. So the youth and the maiden grow up side by side in a life in which the occupations and amusements of the one are so blended with those of the other that they hardly recognize their own distinctness. When they meet after a few years of separation, what strangeness has sprung up between them! Yet across this strangeness they feel their old community of life; and a love comes out of the new relation that perhaps would never have sprung from the old.

Thus does man come at last to find in nature, not merely a condition of his life, not merely a servant, but a companion. He goes to her with all his moods. Nature seems to take them upon herself. She smiles or weeps as man is glad or sorrowful. But in so doing she translates these moods into her own larger life, and the man finds himself calmed or comforted. Thus nature is not only a companion; she is the companion which is the wiser, the more helpful, of the two. She is less the mistress than the wise and tender mother.

We may gain new light upon this matter by glancing at the similar change which the relation of music to the life of man has undergone. In the classic period, music occupied to human life a relation precisely like that held by nature. It was chiefly its accompaniment. Certain styles of music corresponded to certain mental moods or temperaments. These moods the music expressed or stimulated. But in later times man finds between himself and nature the vast chasm of which I spoke. It would seem almost as if he had consciously attempted to fill this chasm by the creation of a new world, a world which should be more like that of the external nature than any other human product, and at the same time more akin to the spiritual world than any merely natural object. Music takes into itself, more than nature can do, the hopes, the fears, the struggles, the aspirations of the human life; but it translates these into a language as universal as that of nature herself. Music is, as I have stated, more akin to the spiritual life than nature is, because it is actually born out of this life; but yet it is as free and universal as nature itself. Thus does it bridge over the chasm between the two worlds.

We have seen that the sense of beauty in nature results from the conscious or unconscious recognition of the community of life between the spirit and the external world. This more or less conscious intuition, or this sense which can hardly be called an intuition, is sufficient to produce a keen enjoyment of natural beauty. As the spiritual life reaches a higher development this relation assumes a higher form ; and the enjoyment of natural beauty undergoes a corresponding change. Byron felt the beauty of nature as keenly as Wordsworth did ; none the less did the enjoyment which Wordsworth found in nature possess higher elements and rise to a calmer and loftier consciousness than that of Byron. The religious soul that is also a lover of nature finds in the life that fills all things the life of God. This change is rather of degree than of kind. The simplest sense of awe and exaltation in the presence of forest and sky is akin to the religious sense ; but yet the conscious identification of the two marks an advance that should be recognized. The religious enjoyment of nature does not, I think, consist in the recognition of contrivance or skill in the various relations of one part of an organism to the rest ; or of one organism to another. Such a recognition may indeed be religious, but it is foreign to the aesthetic sense. This is the really mechanical view of the universe. It makes of it a handiwork, and of the Creator an infinite mechanician. The higher view, or at least the more aesthetic

view, the one I think that we all most naturally
take, regards the universe rather as the manifestation of the divine life than of the divine skill.
The world is born out of the life of God rather
than manufactured by Him.   It is the child
rather than the creature, begotten, not made.   At
first it rests unconscious of the life that is within
it, about it, and above it.   In the human soul it
reaches a higher consciousness.   This recognizes
its Father's love.   It becomes united with God
in a conscious union, and the circle is complete.
The spirit has found that infinite spirit from
which it came.   The circle, I have said, is complete.   In a circle any one point may be reached
from any other by movement in either direction.
Thus the soul may find God by looking backward and feeling itself in the presence of the
universal life that springs from Him, as truly as
by pressing forward to a more conscious and
more absolute recognition of that higher life and
love which are ever leading it on to new and
gladder heights.

We have to take only one step more in order
to complete the survey of the relations that we
are considering.   The lower life of nature being
akin to the highest spiritual life, even while rest-

ing upon a lower plane, is symbolical of that. The last element that meets us of the power which the natural world has over the souls that we rightly judge to be so high above it, is this prophecy which it offers of the highest. Our narrow dissevered human lives, with the limitations, the discords, the weariness that flow from their isolation, lie between two realms of peace. There is the oneness and the peace of the lower nature; there is the oneness and the peace of the higher life of which all perhaps know something, but which yet in its complete perfection rises above the souls that have climbed the farthest. It is the isolation that comes from the separate ends which each is seeking, and from the harsh analysis of the understanding, that gives its prosaic character to our ordinary life, and that severs our human works from the free life of nature. It is, on the other hand, whatever draws each individual out of himself, makes him forget himself and live in other lives, or in the ideal world which forms the absolute life, that changes prose to poetry; that brings man into harmonious relations with nature, and so far fulfils the prophecy which nature has been uttering so long. Men have had a perception of this even in regard to the simplest and most individual form of love. Love is recognized as the romance of life. The forest path has lent itself naturally for its meetings, and the flowers have seemed to find their natural use in becoming its language. This relation between the beauty of nature and the tenderness of love results from the fact that love is self-surrender. In love the individual finds his truest life in the life of another. Thus the narrowness of the individual life is broken through. Its separateness is bridged over. It is no longer prose, but poetry. It has become part of the larger life of nature.

If we turn to the highest aspect of the case, we see more clearly than before why the temple that is the expression of the soul's most perfect abandonment of its own petty limitations, should be so in harmony with the grandest products of the outward world. Thus in these most perfect expressions of the spiritual consciousness are blended the peace of nature, and that higher peace of which this is the symbol and the prophecy.

Our task is thus accomplished. We have not asked why one natural object is fairer than another. We have simply sought to justify, in the

face of all the difficulties that beset us, the love
that we have for nature. We have found this
justification in the fact of the more or less conscious recognition of the freedom of the life of
nature; in that of the identity of our lives with
that of nature; in the fulness of the life of
nature; in its divinity; and in the fact that it
prefigures a perfection which we have not yet
attained. I think that it is from such causes
that we all love nature, each in his degree; and
referring to them, we may cry with Wordsworth,
whose "therefore" rested upon somewhat similar
conditions:—

> "Therefore am I still
> A lover of the meadows and the woods
> And mountains; and of all that we behold
> From this green earth; of all the mighty world
> Of eye and ear, both what they half create
> And what perceive."

THE TRAGIC FORCES IN LIFE AND LITERATURE.

MUCH in life is glad and beautiful, and thus seems well fitted to give pleasure when presented in the form of poetry. It happens, singularly enough, however, that it is the darker and sterner aspect of life which poetry has most loved to represent; or at least, which it has represented with most power. It is in Tragedy that poetic genius has found its most perfect expression. In considering, then, life in its relation to poetry, we naturally turn especially to its tragic elements, and consider the tragic forces as they manifest themselves in literature and in life, and the kind of solution which poetry offers to their mystery.

Our life consists of two elements, which, if they did not mingle in each one of our conscious acts, we should think to be absolutely irreconcilable. These elements in abstract language are named Necessity and Freedom. In theology they take form as law and gospel. In literature they

tend to express themselves respectively in tragedy and romance. I do not mean to draw any
absolute line between the two classes of composition last named. Some romances have the elements of tragedy; some tragedies are romantic.
The tragedy is, however, the natural and more
appropriate as well as more common expression
of those dark forces that underlie our life. Romance presents a solid front of circumstances
and events. The tragedy gives only characters.
The first is like a clock with a painted face, over
which the hands are seen to pass. Tragedy is
like a clock with face removed, showing us the
bare combination of wheels and weights.

If we look more definitely at the nature of
tragedy, the first thing that strikes us is that
in tragedy there is always a collision. The second is that this is a collision of human wills.
The tragedy has to do with humanity. In this it
is like sculpture. The novelist, like the painter,
gives us backgrounds and surroundings. The
dramatic poet, like the sculptor, gives us life.
The dramatist may help out his work by foot-
notes in print, or by scenery on the stage. But
these are foreign to his true sphere. In tragedy,
then, we have the human spirit, stripped like the

athlete, contending with its fellow. The powers of the outward nature may not interfere: they may form a background of terror and sublimity, as in Shakespeare's "Lear;" or of beauty, as in his "As You Like It;" but this is all that they can do. The gods themselves, if they take part, must appear, like the gods of Homer, in the guise and the speech of mortals. This is so, in part, because of the limitation in the material which the dramatist has at his command. But an inward necessity answers to this outward one. The tragedy is the highest form of objective literature, and humanity is its only fitting object. Man is left to fight his own battle. He is placed to rule the world, to trample on nature, or to make her serve his will. He is left single-handed and alone, to conquer his destiny as he can. This sublime and solitary struggle is the theme of the dramatist.

I have said that the tragic collision is a collision of wills. If we use the word "will" to mean simply spiritual force, the phrase is true. But as we look more deeply we see that, though the will is in the foreground, and thus might well appear to be the chief actor, it is in reality the instrument of a power behind itself. Did Othello will to doubt the only being that he loved, and then to slay her? Did Macbeth will to murder the king? And, on the other hand, did not Hamlet will, with all the power that was in him, to avenge his father? The collision in the tragedy, then, is less between wills than between the great forces which act through the wills. The man seems to be self-directed and controlled, but really he is the play of the great powers that are behind him and working through him. He is the bubble on the stream. You look at it and cry, How wildly it hurries on, how gayly it dances, how madly it whirls!—Nay, it is a bubble, that is all. It is the black stream below that drives it and whirls it along its way.

To see more clearly this deeper phase of the tragic element, we must turn to the tragedy of Greece. In the later tragedy other elements mingle with this. Here we shall find it to a large extent pure. In this, these vast and underlying forces are felt more strongly than elsewhere, and may be exhibited more clearly. The music by which the play was accompanied; the stature of the performers, vaster than human; the voice more terrible than human; the great unchanging face, fixed as the marble face of

Jove, fixed in that expression which was the ruling one of the part; the strange choral song
which hovered over all, translating from the individual to the universal, — all of these served to
make the individual the fitting manifestation of
those great forces which acted through him.
And thus we find that the collision in the most
typical Grecian tragedy is the collision of the
great underlying forces of society and of life.
A common form of this collision is that of the
family and of the state.   Such is all that tragic
story of Agamemnon, Clytemnestra, and Orestes.
Agamemnon, at the bidding of the oracle, sacrificed his daughter to his country.   This must be
the offering, the only offering, that should secure
the triumph of the Grecian arms.   The sacrifice
is made and accepted.   Troy falls, the victor
returns in triumph.   But is that the end?   He
had yielded to the power of country, but he had
trampled on that of family and of home.   He had
sacrificed everything to his country.   Very well;
he had his reward; he returned in triumph to
his home, to that home whose dearest laws he
had despised, whose dearest rights he had violated, that home which he sacrificed to his country: shall he triumph there also?   These laws

of family, these forces of home, demand retribution for their despised majesty. They act through Clytemnestra. No harsh and hardened soul was hers, or, if harsh and hardened, it was made so by that power which had torn its true life away. It was fierce, but it was the fierceness of the lion-mother that has seen her whelps hewn to pieces in her presence. Hear her wail, hear her tender reproaches, hear her maintaining by her mother's agony the rights of a mother's love, and you will see the power that slew the returning king, no longer owned as husband, at the bath. But she in her turn had become the offender. The family was right, perhaps, in avenging itself; but it sinned against the state in that it slew the king. Orestes, the prince, must avenge his father's death. His hands become stained with his mother's blood. The family bond knows no more terrible crime than that. He must atone for it. He is haunted by the furies of his mother. Thus the pendulum might swing forever to and fro without rest. Each atonement produces new sacrilege, until a reconciliation is effected by the promise of equal honor to the Eumenides representing the family rights, and Apollo representing the regal dignity.

Another illustration of the collision between the forces of state and family may be found in the "Antigone." The king forbade Antigone to perform the funeral rites of her brother. The state thus violates the sanctity of the family, which demands nothing more absolutely than funeral honors to the departed. Antigone is true to this sanctity, and pays the sad rites to her brother. The family acts through her, but in its turn it defies the state. The king requires her to make atonement by her death. The state thus tramples on the family. Her lover, the king's son, kills himself for grief, and the family is avenged. While neither party is right from the other's standpoint, neither is wrong from its own. Ancient tragedy had something nobler and better to do than to gloat over pictures of mere crime. These powers act to a great extent unconsciously, blindly. This blindness is brought out more distinctly in the story of Œdipus. He kills his father, not knowing who it is; he marries his mother in the same blindness. None the less has he offended against family and state. None the less must he pay the penalty. We can see more clearly how these tragedies represent the working of the great forces which underlie life, if we may assume that Œdipus originally represented the sun-god. As Œdipus slew his father unwittingly, so the sun, by its very necessity, destroys the darkness from which it proceeded. It sinks in the evening into the arms of the purple heaven out of whose bosom it had sprung in the morning; and thereupon it falls into darkness, as Œdipus was plunged into his night of blindness.

If from this point of view we look at our modern tragedy, we shall have a deeper insight than we could have otherwise gained. The difference between the modern and the ancient is that in modern tragedy it is for the most part a nature or a passion that rules and blinds. Othello and Lear were as blind as Œdipus, and as little self-directed. Lear would have the forms of love, and could not recognize it without these forms. Cordelia would have the reality without the forms. Hence the collision and the destruction of both. The tragic character sees only what is right before him on his track. He is like a horse with blinders on each side. His course is marked out from the beginning. His personality has a certain necessary evolution. Whatever the inner law of his being is, he is at the mercy of that.

Generalizing what has been said, it will appear that the three elements which underlie the tragic collision are necessity, blindness, retribution,— a necessity which is that of the underlying forces of life, of the nature itself; a blindness in that this necessity fancies itself free and choosing for itself; a retribution which makes this blindness accountable for whatever it may do; a retribution which is not necessarily the punishment of actual sin, but which may be the atonement that is due to any violated right of any sphere or plane of life; a retribution which is exacted from the higher to the lower, no less than from the lower to the higher.

We have considered the tragic collision as one between different personalities, representing the different forces of life. We have to add to this the conception of a collision both elements of which represent the same character. This may be illustrated by the case in which the collision is between a man's past and his present; when what he would accomplish in the present is confronted and overborne by what he has accomplished in the past. This is an element not infrequent in tragedy, but it is nowhere presented with greater dramatic force and with more terrible reality than in the works of Victor Hugo. We must not let his extravagances blind us to the dark magnificence which underlies them. In the plays of Victor Hugo we have the tragic character vainly attempting to free himself from the tragic fatality which pursues him. This runs through his plays like some grand movement which appears ever under new forms in some great musical composition. I will give one example. Marion de Lorme had lived a life of shame. A pure attachment sprang up between herself and a youth who knew nothing of her past history. She was to him simply Marie, the ideal of womanly purity. She began a new life, and turned her back upon the past. But the past is wrongly named : we carry it into all the concerns of life ; it follows us as our shadows do when we walk towards the sun. Marie was still Marion, ignore it as she might. The black and terrible past was still her past, or rather it was a part of her present. She followed her lover to the prison into which he was cast under sentence of death for some slight offence, cheering and strengthening him by her love. But at last the fearful secret broke upon him. Marie, his pure ideal, was Marion,

the object of his loathing. He repulses her
tenderness. Marion provides a way for him to
escape, and in an agony of supplication urges
him to flee. He resists her entreaties. He
turns coldly from her. But when the hour of
possible escape has passed, and the execution-
ers have come to end his life, he relents. He
presses her to his heart, and breathes words
of love, of reconciliation and forgiveness. But
when she laments their separation, and speaks
of the happiness they might have shared, the
dark necessity unveils itself again. He dashes to
pieces her airy castle. He makes her understand
that, though he can forgive, he cannot forget the
past ; that a free and trusting love could never
have been theirs. In the plays of Victor Hugo
the tragic element reaches its terrible climax.
The tragic character struggles with the destiny
he has drawn upon himself ; struggles up to a
higher plane, but even from that is dragged
back, and made to feel that the past still lives
in him.

These three parts of the tragic elements, necessity, blindness, and retribution, form the great
woof of life. Tragedy did not invent them ; it
found them. I will give two or three historical

illustrations of this tragic element, and will then seek for it in our daily life. The first that I will mention is that of Socrates in his relation to the Athenian state, — a relation which has been pointed out and perhaps exaggerated by Hegel.[1] Socrates represented the great principle of subjectivity. He represented the higher law. His private *daimon* he would trust as he trusted the divine oracles. Thus the principle of Socrates was that of subjectivity. The principle of the Grecian state, whose ideal reaches its climax in the republic of Plato, was objectivity. The individual was swallowed up in the state; law and morality were the same; there was no higher law. The collision was inevitable. This principle of subjectivity was the wedge which was to split open the ancient state. The state divined the presence of that power which was to be its destruction. The comedian Aristophanes brought all the power of his ridicule to bear upon it. The state put the philosopher to death as a corrupter of youth. The comedian and the state were right. The state can recognize nothing higher than itself, and here was a power that

[1] To whom also I am indebted for some of the results of the preceding analysis.

was to destroy it. Socrates was right from the higher plane on which he stood. The state, urged on by the necessity of its own being, blind to the glory of the new life, put him to death. Socrates must by his death make atonement to the injured rights even of the lower sphere.

In the story of Jesus we have the tragedy of the world. He knew himself to be the consummation of Judaism and its fulfilment, and thus claimed the right to be its Christ. The Jews saw that this claim, if allowed, would destroy Judaism. The destruction was to the Jew necessarily the most terrible thing that could occur. The Jew, being a Jew, could see nothing higher than Judaism. For the higher vision he must receive a higher life ; his nature must be changed ; he must be born again, must çease to be a Jew. Thus came the world's tragedy. The collision was inevitable. Jesus died amid the darkness of nature. But the Jew had invaded a higher principle, a higher life, than he dreamed of. Jesus atoned to Judaism with his life ; Judaism made atonement by its terrible destruction. Judaism struck the blow as blindly as Œdipus brought upon himself the guilt of parricide. It was a tragic blindness. "Had they known," cried the apostle, "they would not have crucified the Lord of Glory." It brought its tragic retribution upon itself with equal blindness. The death of Jesus was the end of Judaism, so far as its historic worth and meaning are concerned. The form remained, but the best life had passed out of it. "I, through the law," cried the apostle, "am dead unto the law. I am crucified with Christ." The higher and the lower met. Each invaded the realm of the other; each made atonement to the other, but the higher conquered even by its defeat.

If we turn from the ancient world to the modern, we need not look abroad for examples of this tragic collision. Our own nation has not long ago passed through the tragedy of its history. As it had sinned more deeply than others, because in the presence of greater light, so was its penalty more terrible. Liberty and slavery, united in a single nation, must meet in a life and death struggle.

All the collisions between class and class, that so mark the present, are only instances of the workings of the tragic elements of life. On these, however, we may not dwell, but must hasten to illustrate, in a more general way, the forms which this tragic collision assumes in the relations of our daily life.

The first that I will name is the one that stands lowest in the scale, — one, indeed, that we might hesitate to place in the list. I mean the struggle between the conscious life of man and the blind forces of nature. The hesitation in regard to calling this collision a tragic one arises from the fact that it has properly no place in the tragedy of literature. Here it could be represented only indirectly, and this under the form of chance occurrences, working out good or evil, constituting thus one element of the romance of life. In actual life, however, it is a constant factor. Chances may occur, but the warfare with nature is more fundamental and wide-reaching than all chances. For everything that may be won from her, nature exacts reprisals; yet even by her victory she is conquered. So soon as men learn to obey her, they command her. Thus does the strife continue with varying fortune through each individual life, until at last, to all outward seeming, the forces of nature gain a final triumph, and remain possessors of the field.

A higher form of the tragic collision, and one that more strictly deserves the name, results

from the fact that the individual seeks to exist
for himself and on his own account. He has his
will and his plans. But this will and these plans
the universe does not respect. Other men have
their wills and their plans; the course of history
moves along its appointed way; the individual
must either yield or struggle vainly.

The truest and highest form of the collision,
however, springs from the fact that every man is
partial. Every man is a representative man, and
represents a part and not the whole. Every
man is to a large extent the result of a certain
ancestry, a certain culture, a certain quality of
mind, a certain sphere of life, and a certain habit
of thought. These are the forces that act
through him. His history is largely the evolution of these. These limit his horizon. As I
said of the tragic hero, he is like a horse with
blinders on either side. He sees straight before
him, that is all. Being thus partial·and blind,
he must have collisions, tragic collisions, with
other forces, and for every such invasion he must
make atonement, must suffer retribution. This
is what may be called, in the strictest meaning
of the word, the tragic element of life. On the
other hand, the fact or the dream of natures so

perfectly attuned to one another that they melt into an absolute harmony makes up the highest form of the romance of life.

It must here be noticed that all the tragic forces that underlie our life are good. There is in all nature no power of evil. Thus the animal, the sensual forces, are good. The beast is moved by good and pure forces. But if a man who might live in a higher sphere suffers himself to fall into a lower, suffers these lower forces to work through him, so much the worse for the man. He must suffer the retribution. The forces which manifest themselves in disease are as natural and healthy as those of health itself. But the body that has fallen into their sphere must pay the penalty. The forces of decay, of corruption, of rottenness, are as clean and pure as those of life; only they are lower forces, and woe to the body that sinks down into their realm. Guilt is the suffering of lower forces to act through a medium fitted for the higher. The punishment of guilt is the retribution demanded by the higher. But the lower, if set at naught, claims a retribution no less. The lower sphere, scorned and defied, demands atonement, satisfaction, no less than the higher. The only difference is that its penalties are lower.

I might illustrate what has been said by reference to the diverse qualities of mind. Thus there are men of the reason, and men of understanding. The understanding cannot comprehend the reason. The understanding sees differences, the reason sees identity. The understanding separates, the reason binds. The understanding makes its mock of the reason. It suffers the penalty in its own coldness and blindness and emptiness and loneliness. The reason despises the mere understanding. It bears also a penalty. It has to bear the mockery of the understanding. It is far less a working power in the world. It is not so good a hater, not so good a fighter, and thus finds itself at disadvantage in its own day and generation. We find further illustrations in the different natures that are thrown together in life, — so different that they cannot understand one another, and are continually in some way or other clashing together. Thus there are the brother and sister in that wonderful story, "The Mill on the Floss." Her nature was passionate; his, cold and upright. They could not understand one another. Their love became their grief. He was harsh, and her heart was almost broken, yet neither was conscious of fault or

error.   Who can say why it is that between ·per-
sons thrown together most closely in the world,
brothers perhaps, brought up in the same family,
husband and wife set apart for one another for
a lifetime, there should be such differences?
One impulsive and one cold, one gay and one
quiet, one generous and one niggardly, one radical and one conservative, they cannot understand
one another.   Neither can see how he is to
blame, but somehow life has become a discord
instead of a harmony.   It is darkened by no
crime, but somehow it has become a tragedy
instead of a romance.   This form of the tragic
relation is prominent in the dramas of Robert
Browning.   An example may be found in his
" Luria," where the warm and passionate nature
of the East is brought into contrast with the cold
reason of the West.

   That other aspect of the tragic collision, in
which the individual is confronted and overborne
by his own past, finds abundant illustration in
life.   We set an instrumentality at work, but we
do not know what it will bring about.   So soon
as an influence has gone out from us, we have no
more control over it.   It is no longer our activity.
It is the great powers of nature that we have set

in motion. We cannot stop them, nor guide them. They owe us no subjection. They disown us. If we stand in their way they will crush us as soon as another. Inventors, discoverers, founders, are not in general those who profit by their labors. The power has gone out from them, and will do the bidding of him who can manage it the best. Fiction and history are full of illustrations of this fact. We read of the servant of the magician who set the broomstick to draw water. He could set it in motion, but he knew no power on earth to stop it, and the house was deluged. We read that Ninus, king of Assyria, in a moment of sport, set the crown on the head of his wife Semiramis. Her first and instant command was, "Take this Ninus and put him to death." Rouget de Lisle composed the "Marseilles Hymn." He named it "An Offering to Liberty." Liberty, in the person of the populace, accepted the offering and thrived upon it, and grew wild and reckless and terrible. Rouget de Lisle trembled and fled before it. Liberty, in the shape of the same populace, pursued him still singing, and as he fled the mountain passes echoed with the notes of his own music.

I have thus presented in scattered points and imperfect outlines the tragic elements of life. The tragic collision is the result of no accident. The universal must by its very nature take shape in that which is partial, and the partial is always antagonistic. The universal makes progress only by division and by contention. The state takes form in its parties, the church in its sects, philosophy in its schools. The infinite takes form in the finite. These finite forms clash against one another, perhaps even destroy one another, and are together swallowed up by the infinite, which presses on to clothe itself in higher forms. The great truth is that it is not man, but these great tragic forces which control the world. "Man is free, humanity is bound."—

> "There 's a Divinity that shapes our ends,
> Rough hew them how we will."

I do not say that man may not hasten or hinder. He can neither prevent nor determine. It is much for the man what kind of forces he suffers to work through him. It is much for the drop whether it is borne on by the broad sweep of the current, or eddies off into some muddy pool. To the man it is much, but these forces will sooner or later accomplish their result.

The tragedy, as a work of art, demands repose as well as struggle. If there is collision, there must be at least some hint of the solution of the collision. The philosophic view at which I have just hinted is too vast for its limits. Moreover, the individual is precious to it, and the repose which broods over all must include each individual in its embrace. We have considered the strife ; we must, to complete the survey, glance at the repose in which it is swallowed up.

The most obvious form of this repose is that of success. The hero conquers in the strife. The happiness for which he longs is his. But this lacks the element of necessity, and has no certainty of permanence. Besides, it is not wholly satisfactory. No bauble of worldly success can repay the struggles and anguish of the soul. A deeper form of repose tragedy has sought and found. It is that of death. This is so freely used by tragedy that the word "tragedy" has come to involve the idea of death. What is tragic is supposed to be deadly. Death is supposed to be the culmination of the horror, instead of, as it is so often, the bringer of the peace. We cannot understand the nature of tragedy till we understand the part that death plays in it.

The repose which results from happiness and success lacks necessity and permanence, and thus fails to satisfy our highest æsthetic needs. That of death is free from this lack. It is no accident which might or might not have occurred. It is as certain as fate itself, and awaits the sufferer after the most terrible sorrow. And there is no fear lest it be merely transitory. Fortune may smile or frown, friends may grow weary of remembering, estates may dwindle into nothingness, empires may be overthrown, but this lofty rest remains unbroken : —

> " O earth, so full of dreary noises ;
> O men, with wailing in your voices ;
> O delved gold the wailers heap ;
> O strife, O curse, that o'er it fall, —
> God makes a silence through you all,
> And giveth his beloved sleep."

All at once there is a strange power at work, a strange presence. We are in contact with the infinities and the eternities. A little stroke of the dagger, a little draught of the poison, and there comes down this infinite peace, this eternal silence, in the presence of which the will is dwarfed, and all caprice seems impertinent, and the loftiest and the humblest are alike. All the events of life which had preceded, which were before fleeting and full of change, become now fixed. and statuesque, and partake of the dignity of their close. But, though the events gain in grandeur, the evil of them is almost forgotten. For how contemptible appear all the weariness and care of life in comparison with that lofty repose which is inevitably to succeed them! Our moral sense is satisfied, or at least cannot murmur. There is enough awe and mystery in it to satisfy our feeling of justice towards the guilty; enough peace to console us for the sorrows of the good. We do not need that it should be made terrible, as in the "Faustus" of Marlow, by the presence of demons; nor hallowed, as in that of Goethe's Margaret, by the voice from heaven crying, "*Ist gerettet,*" "Is saved!" We do not need the celestial fruits and flowers which in one of the early dramas the virgin martyr plucks and sends back as a token to her murderers. We have a feeling of awe in the one case, and of peace in the other, which we cannot avoid, and which satisfies all our dramatic need.

Let us observe more minutely the operation of this principle in a single case, that of Shakespeare's Lear. After reading Charles Lamb's essay on the subject, no one can doubt that the death of Lear was, artistically speaking, inevitable. After his sorrows and losses, his sceptre would have been a bauble, and his life full of the ghosts of dead hopes. But an examination will show that the death of Cordelia was equally required by Lear. The misapprehension in the play, which would change at least this part of the result, has arisen undoubtedly from the notion that the suffering of Lear consisted in his exposure and in the loss of his kingdom, and that poetic justice is satisfied by returning these to him again. The longing of Lear, however, is for love. It is the father's heart yearning for an answer of tenderness; and the struggle and plot of the play are in some measure solved when he holds the loving Cordelia to his bosom. But there were three daughters. Where are the two? He loved them all with equal tenderness : how shall the love of Cordelia alone make up the deficiency and fill the great void of his heart? It must be exhibited in such a magnified and exalted form that this one love shall take the place of all. This could only be done by the dignifying and softening power of death. She had died full of love to him, and died a martyr to that love. Love for one could not fill his heart: a loving

sorrow could. His spirit had no longer the elas-
ticity of youth; he could not pass at once from
such terrible agony to joy. A glad love he could
never feel again. A tender sorrow was the nearest approach to happiness that remained to him,
and that was granted him to the full. A horrible tragedy was yet to be enacted about him.
His father's heart must be filled with horror at
the terrible punishment which was to fall upon
his two daughters, unnatural though they were.
Yet this must take place before his death; for
this alone could fitly close the play. The death
of Cordelia supplied what was wanting here also.
He is so occupied with tender grief that he does
not heed the horrors that are going on about
him. He could gain nothing more from life: —

> " He hates him
> That would upon the rack of this tough world
> Stretch him out longer."

But what most gentle messenger should summon him? Does it not seem of all most fitting
that he, who has gone through life sorrowing for
the want of love, should at last die from the surcharged fulness of a loving heart?

But after all, death is the symbol of the real
solution of the tragic conflict, and thus of the

highest repose, rather than the reality. This reality must be found in the spirit itself. Upon this aspect of our subject I can, in conclusion, barely touch; for this true solution, in its highest forms, lies beyond that which is peculiar to tragedy. I will illustrate what I mean by two examples. I have referred to the truly tragic relation of the brother and sister in "The Mill on the Floss." The solution is found in that last moment of insight when their spirits become united in the tenderest love. The collision of their natures had passed; love had destroyed it. The tragic blindness was gone; for love had enlightened them.

A similar solution is found in the "Luria" of Browning, to which I have already referred. He, also, before his death, had an insight into the true relations between the two forms of spiritual life, in which he was able to appreciate that which was most different from his own.

We have seen how, in the tragedies of Victor Hugo, the spirit was continually confronted and overborne by its own past. In the story of Jean Valjean the author deals with the same theme, but plays it out to its magnificent completion. In this, the hero is also dogged by his own past, but when he might have escaped it, when he might have seen it overwhelm another instead of himself, he stepped forward and took the terrible burden upon his own shoulders. It was the tragic retribution, but by this free choice it was transformed. The man was still supreme over his fate.

A dramatic example of the same relation is found in the case of Mildred, in Browning's "Blot on the 'Scutcheon." She forebore all attempt at self-justification; would say and do nothing to palliate her fault; would accept no veneering of it with the forms of respectability; but calmly, though with a broken heart, faced the full consequences of her sin, feeling them to be only its natural and deserved penalty.

Freedom cannot change the nature. It cannot do away with the facts of life; but it can so use them as to change their aspect and meaning. Freedom does not beget freedom, but a higher necessity. The moral principle can exalt the nature till it becomes subject to new influences, as the aeronaut may rise into higher currents; and love may enlarge the nature until it takes the most diverse influence into itself. Resignation and acceptance may take from events their power to harm, even at the very moment of their triumph. That which was most foreign becomes one's own. Thus faith and patience may change defeat into victory, and in the freedom of the pure personality the tragic conflict finds its solution.

II. COMEDY.

THE PHILOSOPHY OF THE COMIC.

THERE are many who would accept nothing which they cannot understand. They believe that the intellect should be the guide of life; that motives should be clearly known in order to be acted upon; in a word, that we should believe, should admire, and should act, simply according to the light that is given us. Experience contradicts such theories, however plausible they may seem. In fact, the best part of our life is that of which we can give no account. Our loftiest emotions, our profoundest beliefs, have always had their roots in the unconscious part of our nature. They have been the result of impulses which have been followed blindly. All this may seem unworthy of that human nature the mechanically complete model of which is thrown off so easily by our philosophers; but perhaps it may imply a deeper and grander view of our own nature, and of the larger nature of which this is a part, than that furnished by these finished and flippant theories. Thus men have always rejoiced in beauty, and bowed themselves before sublimity, and yielded themselves to the stress of the moral sentiment, or submitted humbly to the reproaches of the violated moral sense, and at the same time they have had very little idea what was the meaning of it all. Of course this could not go on indefinitely. It is part of the greatness of our human nature that it strives to comprehend all things. This effort at comprehension is, however, very different from rejecting all that we cannot comprehend. There have been theories of beauty and theories of morality. The joke of it is, — perhaps in consideration of my special theme I may use this phrase, — that these theories have been diametrically opposed to one another, and yet men have felt and acted just as if all had the same theory ; which shows that the theory has had very little to do with the result.

Among those great elements of human nature which have shown themselves to be rooted in the deep, unconscious life of man, must be placed the sense of the ludicrous. Just as men have

bowed before the beautiful, and yielded themselves to the sublime behests of morality, have
worshipped the unseen and uncomprehended ideal
that has seemed the one reality, without being
able to explain or justify their acts, so they have
laughed without being able to tell why, or to say
specifically at what. If you ask almost any person convulsed with laughter what it is that
amuses him so, he will simply point out the
object or repeat the tale. If you ask why he
laughs at it, he will say: "Oh, it is so funny!"
If you ask why it is funny, he can do nothing
but show you again the point of the joke.

Here, too, our philosophers have been very
busy. As they have sought to point out the
essence of beauty and the source of morality,
so they have sought to make the ludicrous trans-
parent to their thought, and we have had theories
of the comic as well as theories of beauty and
of morality.

I have said that, in spite of differing theories,
the great inner, unconscious life goes on its own
way, and men admire and obey and worship and
laugh as if there were no such thing as philosophy. I fear I was not wholly right. I am afraid
that while the theory that a man holds has no

direct influence upon his life, all this theorizing does have a benumbing effect upon the nature. It somehow lowers the vitality. It makes it all seem of less account. One trouble is that we have in these days such a prosaic set of philosophers. Men talk about beauty who seem as if they had never felt a single thrill of æsthetic joy. They write about morality, and seem as if they had never known for a moment what is meant by the stern voice of duty. Men write on style and rhetoric whose clumsy fingers could never form a graceful sentence; and on the comic who seem as if they could never have laughed at a joke in their lives. I confess that all this is depressing. When I felt moved to write upon this theme, of course it was necessary to read, more carefully than I had done before, more or less of the literature of the subject; and in consequence of this, I am now beginning to feel as if a joke were one of the most solemn things in the world. I have gained a new sense from this experience of the manner in which the higher æsthetic, moral, and religious life must suffer from all this prosy platitudinizing.

In spite of this protest, it must be admitted that a true theory of beauty might quicken the power to enjoy; and a true theory of ethics might strengthen the moral nature. I must confess, however, that it is doubtful if a true theory of the comic would help the enjoyment of the ludicrous. We may admire by rule and live by rule, but we shall never learn, at least so I hope and trust, to laugh by rule. A true theory of the comic would, however, throw much light on many relations of the world and life; and, at least, if we must have theories it is better to have them true than false; and this must be the justification of my attempt.

Two principles have been variously recognized as forming the essence of the comic. One is a certain incongruousness in objects or relations. The other is the sudden recognition of some lack or inferiority in others which leads to self-satisfaction in one's own superiority. These two views are obviously not in opposition. The defect which one discovers in another is simply a form of incongruity upon which one can look down with some contempt. Aristotle says that the ridiculous is a certain error and turpitude unattended with pain and not of a destructive nature. The name of Hobbes is chiefly associated with the view that makes the ludicrous suggested by some inferiority. He says: "I may therefore conclude, that the passion of laughter is nothing else but sudden glory arising from some sudden conception of some eminency in ourselves by comparison with the inferiority of others, or with our own formerly; for men laugh at the follies of themselves past, when they come suddenly to remembrance, except they bring with them any present dishonor. It is no wonder, therefore, that men take heinously to be laughed at or derided, that is, triumphed over. Laughter without offence must be at absurdities and infirmities abstracted from persons, and when all the company may laugh together; for laughing to one's self putteth all the rest into jealousy and examination of themselves. Besides, it is vainglory, and an argument of little worth, to think the infirmity of another sufficient matter for his triumph."

The last part of this extract might seem to recognize the fact that there may be laughter without triumph. All that is really meant, however, is to advise that laughter be directed towards absurdities and infirmities in the abstract rather than in the concrete. To carry out the thought a little farther: it is probable that the company thus laughing at infirmities in the abstract are amusing themselves at the weaknesses of human nature in general, above which, in their own fancy at least, they are raised. Their position may be perhaps illustrated by the exclamation of the old lady who cried, " It takes all sorts to make a world, and I thank God I am not one of them."

In our days, Professor Bain has identified himself with the view that makes a certain sense of superiority essential to any perception of the ludicrous. He says : "I quite understand the laugh of pleasure and admiration at a felicitous stroke of wit, but no one confounds this with the genuinely ludicrous." He thus easily defends his position. He lays down a theory of the comic, and denies anything to be ludicrous that does not conform to it. If he could only make the world use words strictly in his sense, all would be well. He, however, incautiously ventures out of this logically safe retreat, and with needless boldness challenges Herbert Spencer, who takes a different view of the matter, to produce an example of a pun that does not involve the idea of degradation. I wonder what he would say to this model little conundrum, which contains a pun, if such a thing exists : "When does English butter become denationalized?" the answer to which is, "When it is made into a little Pat." Here all the joke lies in the patness of the answer, so to speak. One has no contempt for the English or their butter, or even for the little Pat ; and certainly one has only a profound admiration for the maker of the conundrum. Or take another example in which the sense of superiority passes suddenly into its opposite. A well-dressed guest going out of a friend's house falls and rolls down the terraces to the mud at their foot. We are amused at the incident, and it is possible that a sense of superiority enters into our amusement. We are upright, dignified, and clean. We can afford to laugh at this poor fellow scrambling in the dirt. But his friend hearing the noise comes out and cries "What's that?" The fallen guest, hardly yet having reached the soft bed towards which he is plunging, answers, quick as thought,

"'T is ' I, sir, rolling rapidly.' "

All our sense of superiority is gone. Why, this man is the very hero of the pun. He is the martyr of Paronomasia. We feel that if such a test had come to us, we should not have met it as he

did. Our sense of the comic is, however, increased, not lessened, by the admiration.

To prove that the comic does not consist in
the perception of the incongruous, Professor
Bain enumerates many incongruities that he
says may produce anything but a laugh: "A
decrepit man under a heavy burden, five loaves
and two fishes among a multitude, and all unfitness and gross disproportion ; an instrument out
of tune, a fly in ointment, snow in May, Archimedes studying geometry in a siege, and all discordant things ; everything of the nature of disorder, such as a breach of bargain, and falsehood
in general, and also the multitude taking the law
in their own hands ; whatever is unnatural, as
a corpse at a feast, parental cruelty and filial
ingratitude;" he refers also to the entire cata-
logue of the vanities given by Solomon. All
the incidents and classes of incidents referred
to are incongruous, he tells us, but they cause
"feelings of pain, anger, sadness, loathing, rather
than mirth."

Now, even if the ludicrous be the incongruous,
it by no means follows that all incongruity is ludicrous. I venture to say, however, that there is
no one of the incongruities in the list just given

that might not, under some circumstances and to some persons, cause mirth. Take for instance the case of the decrepit old man under a burden. To the street boy, how many old men have been the subject of mockery, from Elisha down! While an instrument slightly out of tune might not excite mirth, I think that a sudden and gross discord in the midst of harmony often provokes a smile. Such is the sudden squeaking out of a leaking organ-pipe at the wrong place. I was once in a carriage with a company of singers who had just taken part in a funeral service, and was not a little shocked when they burst into laughter while still in plain view from the house of mourning. Something had gone wrong with the music, and in spite of the dictum of Professor Bain, it was ludicrous to them. Why Archimedes studying geometry in a siege should have been placed in the list of objects that "cause feelings of pain, anger, sadness, and loathing," I do not understand. To the thoughtful mind it suggests rather a sense of sublimity. There are, however, persons to whom this would seem, or might be made to seem, one of the most absurd things in the world. The absorption of the man of books, in the midst of the in-

terests and perils of ordinary life, has often been
the theme of jests. The ancient philosopher
who, while gazing at the stars as he walked, fell
into a ditch, may stand as an example of this
collision between the speculative and the practical mind. The absent-mindedness of the student
or the thinker has always been found ridiculous,
as in the *Scholastikos* of the Greek reader. I
need not go through the list. I will give simply
an extreme case, more extreme than any which
has been referred to. The murder of one's grandmother is certainly one of the most awful things
in the world; but in Andersen's story of "The
Great Klaus and the Little Klaus," the fact that
the great Klaus was entrapped into killing his
grandmother, in the hope of obtaining a great
price for the body of the old lady, is one of the
funniest points of the narrative.

The fact that the most painful incidents may
be made matter of mirth brings us face to face
with an absurd difficulty, the reality of which we
could hardly have guessed in advance. I mean
the difficulty of distinguishing between the
comic and the tragic. Indeed, when we look at
the matter we see that there is a very close connection between the two.

The circumstances which suggest the comic are very naturally those which are, to a greater or less extent, really tragic. The tragic is, like the comic, simply the incongruous. The great tragedy of nature, which is called the Struggle for Existence, results simply from a greater or less incongruousness between any form of life and its surroundings. Thus it is that there is nothing tragic that may not to some persons, or to some moods, be comic. Take the great tragedies themselves. Take the story of Œdipus: A man goes forth and meets another, whom he does not know, and kills him; this stranger turns out to be his father. He falls in love with a woman that he meets, and marries her; she proves to be his mother. Shall we have out of all this a tragedy or a comedy? This depends upon the taste of the author, or of the audience for whom he writes. Or take the story of Clytemnestra. How many comedies have found their motive in domestic infidelity! What can be more tragic, more wholly sad, than the thought of a mother waiting and watching for her son who does not come? He is lying all the while among the dead. He has fallen in battle, and that waiting mother shall never greet her child

again. Yet to the Israelites, the thought of the
mother of Sisera looking through her lattice,
and wondering why her son delayed his coming,
presented a picture irresistibly ludicrous. Thus,
in barbarous or semi-barbarous warfare, the victor mocks his fallen foe and laughs at his sufferings. In lands called civilized and Christian,
how many are there who make merry over the
misfortunes of those who have offended them ;
sometimes even over those of persons who are
indifferent to them ; or even those of their
own friends! These examples are enough to
show that the distinction which from Aristotle
downward philosophers have sought to make
between the tragic and the comic, by which incongruity without pain is regarded as comic, and
incongruity accompanied by pain as tragic, has
no existence. The greatest suffering connected
with any incongruity is not enough to take away
its comic aspect to many minds.

If it is true that there is nothing tragic that
may not, to persons in certain grades of moral
development or in certain moods, become comic,
it is equally true, on the other hand, that very
much of the comic has its tragic side. The
tragic collision may be to most, perhaps to all,

unimportant, yet it is real, and we can imagine circumstances under which it might be keenly felt. In my student days I was strolling with classmates by the side of a broad ditch that was half filled with muddy water. "You cannot jump over that, Jones," said one to another. In a moment Jones felt himself put upon his mettle. Before we fairly knew what he was doing, he was half across the ditch ; but, alas! only half. As he emerged dripping, his boots and clothing covered with mud, you can imagine the laughter that greeted him. The formula of the joke was precisely that of the mirth which the savage finds in the sufferings of his fallen foe. In each case, the comic consists in the incongruity between the ill-founded hopes, the conceit with which the man set forth, and the ridiculous failure of it all. The savage thinks, "He came out against me, he was going to destroy me, and lo ! here he is, caught in his own trap, fallen into his own ditch." Unwittingly I have stumbled into the ditch which caused the laugh against poor Jones. Suppose, however, that he had been the son of a widow, who had toiled early and late that he might appear respectably among his comrades. She had felt a mother's pride when

he went forth elegant in his new and shining
suit. Would she see the joke, do you think,
when he came home, his fresh garments drag-
gled and spoiled? We students saw the comic
side; there was also a tragic side, which under
certain circumstances would have been keenly
felt. Or suppose him to have had a consumptive
tendency: in this case the tragedy would have
been yet more keen.

We read Mrs. Caudle's curtain lectures, and
find them very funny. To poor Caudle they
were not all fun.. We make merry over Jack Fal-
staff. Was there no tragedy there? Prince Hal
laughed at the comedy. King Henry saw the
full force of the tragedy. Who so funny as Dog-
berry? His blunders and his stupidity are irre-
sistible. But suppose him to have a daughter
who had been to the schools, who knew that " va-
grant" was not pronounced " vagrom," who had
been proud of her father's appointment, and had
hoped for a certain social elevation from it, and
was proportionally mortified at the exhibition he
was making of himself; or suppose a reformer to
have been present who was indignant that such
men should hold office, would he not have cried,
" Yes, write him down an ass; and when you do

this, you write down the government that appointed him an ass; and you write down an ass every citizen that does not protest against such misuse of government patronage." Neither of these would see the joke.

We thus find that it is very difficult to determine what kind of incongruity is ludicrous. The examination has brought to light the fact that the standard of the comic varies with different individuals. In cases where one man would be shocked, or in those where one would be filled with awe, another would be moved to uproarious laughter. This might suggest to us to seek for the source and measure of the comic within rather than without.

It would be interesting to know if considerations like those that have been named were in the mind of Socrates when he insisted upon the kinship between comedy and tragedy. If only his companions had not at the important moment begun to doze, "as not very well following the argument," we might, perhaps, have found the whole substance of this discussion set forth in the "Symposium." The saying of Socrates, that "He who is by art a tragic poet is also a comic one," is a remarkable prophecy of Shakespeare,

to have been uttered when the lines between the
two kinds of composition were so sharply drawn
as they were in Greece. At the same time we
must not accept this proposition too literally.
The more the comic collision may resemble the
tragic one, the greater must be the difference
between the points of view, or the moods of
mind, from which comedy and tragedy respectively spring, and it is not every poet that can
assume indifferently the one or the other. The
relation of Socrates to the Athenian state formed,
as we have seen, the tragedy of Greece; but the
fate of Socrates was the legitimate outcome of
the comedy of Aristophanes.

Schopenhauer is, I think, the only writer who
has laid a real foundation for the philosophy of
the comic, though it is only a foundation. Before discussing the nature of the comic, he had
been discoursing upon the human reason. The
reason is to him the power of thinking by conceptions more or less abstract. The process
of thought consists in forming generalizations;
or in the subsumption of particular and individual objects and events under more general conceptions. The sense of the ludicrous
is caused by certain aspects or results of this

process of subsumption. Thus, when an individual object is put by us into some category
where there is a certain reason for placing it, but
where for many other reasons it is strikingly out
of place, we may have the sense of the ludicrous.
The more reasonable on the one side is the subsumption of this particular object under this
general conception, and the greater and the
more glaring on the other is its unfitness for
this generalization, so much the stronger is the
comic effect that springs from it. We should add,
what Schopenhauer overlooks, that this subsumption is the play of the imagination rather than
the act of the conscious intellect. A like result
is produced by a word in which dissimilar meanings are united. When of two meanings one forces
itself upon us that is strikingly out of place, we
may have the sense of the ludicrous.

It will be noticed that I say "we may have the
sense of the ludicrous," not that we shall have
it. Not every such generalization, not even
every glaring extravagance of the kind, produces
a comic effect. There must be a special degree
of fitness united with a special degree of unfitness; and the two must stand in a special
relation to one another, if the effect is to be

produced. Whether these conditions are or are not fulfilled cannot be determined by the application of any rule. No *a priori* reasoning can be applied to the matter. A joke, in its way, is like a piece of music or a statue. Beauty is a matter, not of reasoning but of recognition. We may have a fine philosophy of art, but its use is in explaining success rather than in prophesying it. The philosophy may be good, but the elements in the æsthetic effect are too delicate for scientific forecast. All this is true also of the joke.

Schopenhauer errs, I think, when he divides the comic into two classes. In the one class he places the witty conceit, and in the other the foolish act. In the first case, we consciously bring foreign and heterogeneous elements under some higher generalization to which their unfitness is manifest. In the second case, a man starts with a conception which he proceeds to apply to the outer world, taking it for granted that the outer world will conform to it; but when he finds that things do not respect his preconceived idea, and all turns out quite opposite to what he had expected, he is filled with astonishment. As an instance of this, Schopenhauer

tells of two peasants who wished to remove the
shot from their gun without firing it. One puts
the muzzle of the gun into his hat, and his hat
between his knees, and tells the other who holds
the gun to pull the trigger " gently, gently, gently, and the shot will roll out." This he says,
proceeds from the general notion that a retarding
of the cause will produce a corresponding result
in the effect. I quote this, not as being so very
funny in itself, but as suggesting a comic aspect
to some of the popular speculation of the day.
This goes on precisely the opposite assumption,
though one wholly kindred in fact ; namely, that
the more slowly a result is produced, the more
can a cause be dispensed with. Those who reason thus do not realize that as much force is
expended in rolling a ball slowly up hill as if it
were rolled rapidly. Thus any human faculty,
for instance, is supposed to be accounted for
when the stages of its very prolonged development have been pointed out.

I think that Schopenhauer is wrong in making
out of folly and blundering a special type of the
ludicrous. If it be thus specially classified, it
should not be opposed to wit, but should be one
of the classes of objects which wit can use. A

blunder in itself is not funnier than anything else. It may be contemplated with stern seriousness, as by a schoolmaster. The comicality comes when we unite, in our conception of the man, the self-confident assumption of wisdom and the absolute ignorance of the facts of the universe, or thoughtlessness in regard to them.

Schopenhauer's explanation of the pleasure which we derive from the comic shows that the one form of it which he appreciates is that of blundering, pedantry, and the like, which he puts into the second class. It is the pleasure we take in seeing that hard task-mistress, Reason, the source of our cares and our sorrows, proved inadequate by the perception, which is the source of our spontaneous pleasures. This is quite in the spirit of Schopenhauer's philosophy; but it depends wholly upon the person which of the two sides of this contrast shall be found ridiculous. If to one it is the reason that is ludicrous, because it mistakes the fact, to another it is the fact which does not conform to the reason. Emerson, for instance, takes this second view. In his admirable essay on the comic he says: " The best of all jokes is the sympathetic contemplation of things by the understanding, from the

philosopher's point of view.   There is no joke so
true and deep in actual life as when some pure
idealist goes up and down among the institutions
of society, attended by a man who knows the
world, and who, sympathizing with the philosopher's scrutiny, sympathizes also with the confusion and indignation of the detected skulking institutions.   His perception of disparity, his eye
wandering perpetually from the rule to the
crooked, lying, thieving fact, makes the eyes run
over with laughter."   It is like the story of Don
Quixote, in which every one finds something ludicrous, though different persons would be found
laughing at opposite sides of the same contrast.
One illustration given by Schopenhauer in another connection may illustrate this.   I will venture to translate the German couplet into English, thus : —

> " Our parson 's the good Shepherd of whom the Bible spake,
>   His flock all soundly sleeping and he alone awake."

One, in such a picture as this, would find the
idea of the good pastor made ridiculous.   He
would say : " You have had your fine ideal ; here
you see what is the real fact."   Another would
hold fast to his ideal.   It would be to him more
true and more precious than ever.   His ridicule

would be directed simply against the poor sham who found himself suddenly surrounded by the light of the true ideal of the position he had usurped. My own belief is that, although one may find one side of a contrast ridiculous, and another the other, the ludicrous itself is something entirely apart from this whole aspect of the case. The ludicrous is simply the incongruity between the elements which we bring under a single generalization, or the incongruity of any one fact with the generalization under which we would bring it. The contempt which one person or another may feel in regard to one side or another of the contrast has nothing to do with the comic as such. The comic itself, like a lambent flame, may play over the surface of things without scorching them. If the power to burn be, as it often is, associated with this, it is as a distinct element.

If the comic is a result of a certain kind of generalization, it would follow that there is absolutely no such thing as the comic in nature. The comic is purely subjective : there is no objective element whatever. It is purely a matter of generalization and subsumption.

It is a matter of classification, and there are

no classes in nature. Everything is once for all what it is. Anything becomes comic only when we mentally place it in relations, or into categories, where it appears out of place. What is true of nature is, with a single exception, true of life. The exception is found in the fact that there is in life such a thing as the farce. Persons may put themselves in relations knowing that they are ridiculous, and for the purpose of being ridiculous. That is, the human individual may be comic to and for himself. With this exception it is as true of life as of nature that the comic, objectively considered, does not exist. A blunder is a blunder ; a foolish person is an individual with certain endowments and at a certain stage of development. He may seem ridiculous when we compare him with something that he is not.

Nature plays. The beauty of the world represents this play. The animals play. Even the busy ants, we are told, refresh themselves by games after the work of the day is done. They have their trials of strength, their wrestling matches, as it were. Play is, however, something very unlike the comic. A game of chess, or even a well-played game of base-ball, is not a funny spectacle. Whether any of the higher animals ever pass the line that separates play from jest, I will not here attempt to decide. Perhaps the nearest approach to this may be found in the teasing of one animal by another. If it be proved that the animal may jest, the nature of the comic is not thereby changed. It is still a matter of contemplation or creation. The only difference is, that the animal has passed from the ring to the spectator's seat.

We may now see that the distinction made by Professor Bain between the witty and the ludicrous is worse than artificial. It is wholly false. There is nothing comic but wit. When we laugh at anything, we " make fun " of it.

We may see now, from a new point of view, the difference between the comic and the tragic. Tragedy may, be what the comic cannot be, an outward fact. Man may behold it and may be moved by it ; but it does not ask from any such recognition ieave to be. It existed long before man appeared upon the earth. The great struggle for existence, which is recognized so widely as the moving power of development, contains the essence of tragedy. In it an individual, shaped by one combination of natural forces, is brought into collision with a different combination of forces. Innumerable individuals are brought into sharp collision with one another. The competition for life is a tragic struggle. In human history tragedy is something real, whether spectators do or do not watch with eagerness its course, and exult with the victor or mourn for the fallen. But comedy must be seen in order to exist. It is created in the mind of the beholder.

This truth in regard to the comic may be illustrated by innumerable examples. Indeed, there is not a comic object that might not serve as proof. I will refer to a very few examples that may make the meaning of what has been said clear, and may give an intimation of the kind of analysis by which it may be supported.

If anything in nature is in itself comic, it would be found among those objects which are surrounded in the mind by comic associations, and which have a comic aspect to persons in themselves widely different, and to those widely separated in time and space. This association with the comic we naturally transfer to the object itself, and regard that as in itself ludicrous. Perhaps nothing in nature has been honored with the laughter of such diverse and widely separated peoples as the frog. Greece shook its sides over this little batrachian. We need think only of the so-called Homeric hymn of " The Battle of the Frogs and the Mice," and of the tragedy of Aristophanes to which the frogs give the title.

The fact that in the Vedic hymns also the frog figures in a comic capacity is, perhaps, less familiar. A burlesque hymn is addressed to the frogs. The repetition of the same sound by one frog and another is compared to the repetition by a pupil of the speech of his teacher. After quite a detailed description the hymn closes as follows : —

" Like Brahmins at the Soma sacrifice, . . . sitting round a full pond and talking, you, O frogs, celebrate this day of the year when the rainy season begins. . . . Cownoise gave, Goatnoise gave ; the brown gave and the green gave us treasures. The frogs, who give us hundreds of cows, lengthen our life in the rich autumn." [1]

The comparison of this poem with the treatment of the frog in Greek literature is instructive. In each the object of mirth is placed in a category where it does not belong. This category varies with the habits of the different peoples. In the Homeric hymn the chief element of the comic is found in the fact that the frog

[1] This quotation is taken from a translation by Max Müller.

figures as a warrior. In the Vedic hymn the point of the joke is in making the frog figure as a Brahmin. The joke of making the frogs appear as warriors is based simply on their absolutely unwarlike character. The making them figure as Brahmins had more point. Their monotonous cries might probably take off very well the drone of the priest; while the endless repetition of the same sound formed a very good caricature of the manner in which teacher and pupil would go over the same hymn, forward and backward, with utter disregard of the meaning. Besides these special conceptions of warrior and priest, there are others more general, in connection with which the frog may appear ludicrous. Our notion of a living creature is one which must include the frog, but yet the little clump is very far from our ideal of life. In spite of all this sport made of it by such widely sundered nations, the frog is no joke. It is a peaceable little creature just adapted to its surroundings.

A toad is not a frog, but the resemblance is so close that I will quote a graceful poem by Edgar Fawcett on the toad. This will illustrate still further the fact that the ludicrous depends upon some form of comparison or generalization.

"Blue dusk, that brings the dewy hours,
    Brings thee, of graceless form in sooth,
Dark stumbler at the roots of flowers,
    Flaccid, inert, uncouth.

"Right ill can human wonder guess
    Thy meaning or thy mission here,
Gray lump of mottled clamminess,
    With that preposterous leer !

"But when I meet thy dull bulk where
    Luxurious roses bend and burn,
Or some slim lily lifts to air
    Its frail and fragrant urn,

"Of these, among the garden ways
    So grim a watcher dost thou seem,
That I, with meditative gaze,
    Look down on thee and dream

"Of thick lipped slaves with ebon skin,
    That squat in hideous, dumb repose,
And guard the drowsy ladies in
    Their still seraglios."

With us the jackass is more generally found ludicrous than the frog. The comicality of this animal also results from our habit of generalization. I think I never see an ass without wondering afresh that it is so small. It is certainly very small and gentle when compared with its voice. It seems to be tied to its voice as Cicero's nephew to his sword. The voice certainly seems too much for the poor beast. How it wrestles with it! It seems to be struggling to pump it up from some unknown depth. It pumps and strains; but just as we think the work is done and the voice will come forth clear and strong, down it goes, and the whole thing must be done over again. Its ears are as much too large for it, judged by any common standard, as its voice. "Nursey dear," cries the little girl, contemplating its aural appendages, — "Nursey dear, do you think it would hurt it if I should touch its wings?" And yet, gentlest and, unless thy grave looks belie thee, wisest of quadrupeds, I would not be thought to cast ridicule upon thee. On the contrary, I am simply showing that when we laugh at thee, it is only at foolish fancies of our own that we laugh. Thy voice, thine ears, thy wise look, all become thee, all serve their purpose, and if we take thee by thyself, thou art no more ludicrous than the gazelle.

But surely, it may be urged, the monkey is ludicrous in itself. The comicality of the monkey consists solely in the fact that it is such a carica-ture of humanity. The monkey seems like such

an absurd little old man, and the maternal discipline which we see in the monkey's cage so re-
minds us of what we sometimes see in human
life, that the effect of the resemblance and the
difference is charmingly comical.

If we pass from the world of the lower nature
to that of human life, the same principle holds
good. Take as an example one of Mark Twain's
stories. There were two sisters, one a wife and
one a widow. A friend long absent returns to
the city where they live. He looks into the
crowded court-house and finds the living husband
pleading a case, and burdened by heat and weariness. As he comes out and strolls along the
street, he sees the widowed sister in a café, eating an ice. He joins her and calls for an ice.
As he sips it he thinks of the poor lawyer he had
just left, and mistaking the widow for her sister,
and thinking her the lawyer's wife, he exclaims:
" Madam, if your husband could only have a
little of this ice in the intolerable heat where he
is now suffering!" Her look shows him his
mistake, and he flees precipitately from the place.
This was a simple mistake like any other, only
so much worse than many another. It becomes
ludicrous when we apply to it our notions of the

shockingly inappropriate and the shockingly appropriate, and try to unite both in our conception of the scene; we think of the pleased sense of the man at having thought of the polite thing to say, and of his disgust at having been so grotesquely impolite. We .picture the confusion of his mind, divided between the heat of the court-room and that other heat. All these various elements are taken into our thought of the man or of the event, and the formula of the comic is fulfilled; namely, we have incongruous elements united in a single general conception.

We may illustrate the same point by the story of the German professor who was wondering that his lecture-room was so empty. Forty or fifty years ago, he says, the room was crowded. It is perfectly inexplicable to him, especially as he reads precisely the same lectures now that he did then. Here we have in our thought the reason why he ought to succeed and the reason of his actual failure brought together under one general principle, namely, the sameness of his lectures. Perhaps we may complete the confusion of the thought, by adding to it the mingled venerableness and absurdity of a general custom which this particular professor was following.

The result of all this is the fuller recognition
of the fact already stated, that the comic lies not
in the thing, but in our way of looking at it.

In transferring the comic from the objective
to the subjective world, Schopenhauer has certainly made a very important advance, and we
might think that the difficulties were wholly
solved. Practically they remain as great as ever.
The distinction is really of less importance than
it seems. The fact is that the outer world, as it
exists for us, is practically the result of our own
processes of thought. We see nothing in its
bare isolation. Our most real objects are embodied categories or classes. Thus the comic,
though subjective, is no more so than many of
the solid facts with which we contrast it. The
comic ordinarily seems to us as truly objective
as the tragic ; and the tragic is often, though not
always, the pure result of imagination, and thus
as subjective as the comic. Thus the difficulty,
however absurd, remains.

We need, then, to seek some formula for the
comic which shall define it more accurately, and
shall enable us to distinguish, in theory as readily
as in fact, between the comic and the tragic. I
will venture to suggest a formula that appears to

me to contain more truth and to be more helpful in this respect than any that I have seen. It is this : both the comic and the tragic are based upon incongruities ; the difference between them lies in the fact that the comic is found in an incongruous relation, considered merely as to its *form*, while the tragic is found in an incongruous relation taken as to its *reality*. By the *form* I mean the simple relation of incongruity. By the *reality* I mean the elements that enter into the relation, the causes that produced it, and the effects which result from it. So far as the causes are concerned, these belong to the realm of science, and to science nothing is ludicrous. By the effects which result from it, I mean the destruction and the sorrow when these are regarded sympathetically. Nothing is comic to the heart. Thus the comic may be regarded as the froth and foam of life. If it be urged against this illustration that the comic is often associated with our deepest experiences, it must be answered that the most profound disturbance of the ocean may produce the most abundant froth and foam.

In real life, form and reality are inseparable : thus the tragic has a real objective existence.

The form can be separated from the reality only by a process of thought; thus the comic is, as we have seen, purely subjective.

The difference between what I have called the form and the reality of a relation may easily be made clear. Why does the crowd that watches a Punch and Judy show laugh at the beatings which Punch gives to Judy, when in real life such an exhibition would ordinarily arouse their indignation? It is simply that in the case of Punch we have merely the form, the appearance, of wife-beating, to which the reality is wholly wanting. In real life it is sometimes possible to make a similar abstraction; to witness a transaction that has its painful side with no more sense of its reality than we have in the exhibition just described. This may be illustrated by any of the examples that have been referred to. When the man emerged muddy and dripping from the ditch, the form of the relation is the contrast between the conceit with which the action began and the downfall that followed it. The reality consists in the ruined clothes and the possibility of impaired health. It is possible to look at the former of these without any thought or sense of the latter; to regard it with no more sympathy than we might feel for such a catastrophe in a theatre. Looked at in this way, the thing is simply ludicrous. So soon as our sympathy or our anxiety go beyond the outward seeming, and make us feel something of the loss, suffering, or peril, then the comic aspect of the thing is lost.

THE PHILOSOPHY OF THE COMIC.

(*Continued.*)

In our study of the comic, we have thus reached certain principles that must be regarded as fundamental. We will now proceed to apply these to various aspects of the comic. They will perhaps throw light upon certain matters that have been the theme of much discussion.

One of these is the distinction between wit and humor. Wit entirely separates the form from the reality. It cares not whether, in making this separation, it does or does not leave a smarting wound. Humor feels a deep sympathy with the reality, a sympathy which would seem to render the sense of the ludicrous impossible. Its regard and its sympathy are, however, so strong, that the form which it tenderly separates seems wholly superficial. It holds the form distinct, and laughs at it; but through this, and behind it, it sees and loves the individual that furnishes the content. In other words, this particular form is so superficial that it may separate itself, leaving the substance whole and uninjured. Take, for instance, the treatment of some of his characters by Dickens. He sees the comical side of them, but yet he knows that this is not all, and loves them. Poor, awkward, ugly Kit Nubbles! Another might have left him so, and we should have laughed, not merely at his peculiarities, but at himself. Dickens, however, knows that he has so true and loving a heart that he can afford to be ugly and awkward. So was it also with Dora. What a little fool she was, to be sure! Yet we love her as if she were the most sensible person in the world. The difference in treatment Dickens himself may illustrate. When he wrote the story of Dora, the picture that he drew was full of humor only. He laughed about Dora, but not at her. When he read the story in public he was, or seemed to be, out of sympathy with his own creation. I confess myself to have been pained at hearing him and the audience laughing, not merely about poor Dora, but at her. Thus we may understand the jests that friends make about one another, the friendly rallying in regard to some little peculiarity. We understand, too, how smiles and tears often contend with one another, or amicably divide the field between them.

Another question that has been more or less discussed is, how far ridicule may be made a test of truth. From what has been said, it will appear that it is in no sense or degree such a test. There is nothing, however true or however sacred, that may not be made ridiculous to some minds. All that is necessary is some absurd classification in which the object to be ridiculed shall be put into incongruous relations. The comic may furnish the test, not of truth, but of the reality, and above all, of the intensity of feeling in the person who is affected by the ludicrous aspect of any object or event. Not even a man's admiration betrays his inner nature more truly than his laughter. We have seen that humor may make itself merry with absurdities connected with persons who are really held dear; there is a point, however, where this merry-making must stop, a line beyond which laughter would give place to pain or anger :-

> " Though men may bicker with the things they love,
> They would not make them laughable in all eyes,
> Not while they loved them."

Even a devout person may be amused at some inappropriate incident accidentally occurring in a church service; while if such an incident had been arranged out of a spirit of mockery, he would be shocked. An interruption at which one would smile if it had happened during an ordinary church service, would give keen pain if it occurred during the funeral of some dear friend. These examples may illustrate the fact that the test furnished by the comic is subjective rather than objective; that it applies to the nature or feelings of the person who laughs, and not to that which is found laughable.

The results that have been reached may explain the great gain that comes to any life from the sense of the ludicrous. One gain is obvious, indeed, without study : the sense of the ludicrous will do much to keep a man from "making a fool of himself." It will not wholly prevent the possibility of ridicule. One may still do or say seriously what will be turned into joke; but he will not be at fault. Take, for instance, that line of Tennyson in which, speaking of Geraint, he says : —

"For now the wine made summer in his blood."

It is not the fault of the poet if it occurs to me

in reading that Geraint must have drunk freely,
because "one swallow does not make a summer."
The sense of the ludicrous will, however, prevent
a man from saying and doing what others will
find ludicrous in spite of themselves. That men
and women do this is familiar in the experience
of us all. My mind is full of examples of this
kind as I write ; but I refrain from introducing
them, lest haply these pages should fall under the
eyes of the persons concerned. Meanwhile the
series in "Punch" of "the things one would
rather have left unsaid" may be referred to in
illustration. I will cite specially one of the heroes of "Punch," though not, I believe, connected
with this series, who, showing a friend through
his house, introduces him at last to a retired
library. "Here," he exclaims, "I can sit and
study by the hour together, and nobody any the
wiser."

The advantage that has been named is, however,
merely relative. It shows that, since the world
in general has a sense of the ludicrous, any individual who may be destitute of it finds himself at
disadvantage. It does not throw light upon the
gain that comes to mankind in general from the
possession of this gift. The view that has been

taken in this discussion of the comic in general·
will, however, make this clear; we have seen that
in the comic we have to do with the form of a relation, and not with its reality. The weariness of
life comes from our subjection to the stern realities of things. We are slaves to the substance.
The comic brings rest and refreshment, because
by it we are released from the grip of the substance, and taken into the realm of pure forms.
The sense of the beautiful brings rest, because
in æsthetic enjoyment we are taken out of all
personal relations, and placed in a state of pure
contemplation. We are still, however, serious
and earnest. The sense of the comic is produced by the contemplation of the incongruous ;
that of beauty, by the contemplation of the harmonious. Beauty we feel, however, to represent
the reality of things, while in the comic we do
not look beyond the surface. Thus, while both
the comic and the beautiful refresh us, the comic
leaves us simply refreshed. Beauty may bring
to us inspiration for a higher life.

In the comic we are taken into the world of
surfaces. The forms about us mean nothing.
All is empty. We are wholly free from the substance and are refreshed. Thus Shakespeare,

when our mind is most strained by sympathy, takes us suddenly into the world of pure forms. The too intense mind becomes relaxed by this play of the comic. When we return to the world which he has created for us, the mind, relieved of its tension, can give itself with fresh interest to the events that pass before it. Mere negation of substance, mere vacuity, mere aimlessness, would be tedious. But the comic brings occupation that is not business. We have the form though the substance is missing. We have emptiness that is not vacuity ; a definite aimlessness ; a disorder that preserves the form of law.

We can now understand the place which the sense of the ludicrous fills in the constitution of the mind. There are persons almost wholly destitute of it. Such persons are tied down to the substantial facts of life, whether these be important or unimportant. I will not say that they suffer more than those who have the sense of the ludicrous ; for the power of the imagination that goes with this may sometimes create sorrows. They are, however, hard and wooden. Intercourse with them is like driving in a wagon without springs. The perception of the comic implies the power of separating the form from the substance. It implies the possibility of emanci-pating one's self from the realities that would hold us down to their routine. One who sees the ludicrous side of everything lives in a world of empty forms. Thus the poet sings of the "loud laugh that speaks the vacant mind." A mind wholly given to the ludicrous would be wholly vacant. That man is happily constituted who can take serious things seriously, but who, in a thousand little matters which might disturb his peace, can take the form for the substance, and laugh where he might otherwise weep. Thus a natural, hearty laugh is at once a sign of san-ity and a preserver of it. One who can laugh naturally is for the moment free from any *idée fixe* that may be haunting him. He shows, for the moment at least, a superiority to the hard facts of life. The smile that one feels obliged to cast about him as he picks himself up after an awkward fall is a tribute to the world's sense of the worth and the meaning of this power to take the form of the relation instead of the hard, underlying fact which is so obvious in this particular case. He who has not this power of laughter, even at the awkwardnesses and the un-comfortablenesses that may beset his own path, is only half equipped for the experiences of life.

The question as to the cause of the pleasure which we take in the contemplation of the incongruities that have been illustrated, is, perhaps not wholly to be answered. Sooner or later we reach certain ultimate facts in our constitution, that must be accepted without further explanation. This may be one of them. Yet one or two considerations may be suggested that will throw a little light upon the matter. I conceive that there may be found some help in the reference that Schopenhauer, as we have seen, makes to the "hard task-mistress Reason." The special use made by Schopenhauer of our relation to this hard task-mistress is based upon a misapprehension ; but the relation itself may help us a little way in our present search. In the comic our spirits find a sphere of pure play. We have a sense of freedom. We have escaped from the control of our task-mistress. But the joy of freedom is never felt so keenly as in the shadow of our servitude. In the comic we are not only free from the rule of reason : we play with the rule itself. We are like the schoolboy who, armed with the spectacles and the rod of the master, exerts a mimic authority. It is by the very process of generalization, through which our science and our philosophy are so laboriously built up, that we erect the unsubstantial fabric of the ludicrous. By another form of illustration, the comic may be compared to a saturnalian revel, in which the master, reason, serves. To this emancipation from reason even while we are using the forms of reason, which is implied by the comic, should be added that other emancipation that has been before described; that, namely, from the solid relations of life. These considerations may help us a little way in understanding the pleasure that we derive from the ludicrous. I do not claim that they do more than this, and admit that the heart of the mystery is probably untouched.

The relation between the perception of the comic and laughter raises interesting questions. The connection is not an invariable one. We certainly do not always laugh at what we feel to be ludicrous, and, on the other side, there is the laughter of pleasure, of conceit, and of surprise. In regard to these latter forms of laughter, while I do not wish to be dogmatic in the matter, I am inclined to think that all laughter, except that having a purely physical cause, is suggested by some relation similar to that which has been described. This relation may not have a really comic aspect, even to the person who laughs. In it, however, incongruous elements are brought together under some single generalization. It thus is of the nature of the comic, though the incongruities may not be sufficiently pointed for true comic effect. Take, for instance, the laugh of triumph when one has solved a puzzle or any difficult problem. The incongruity of the elements that enter into the puzzle has been impressed upon us so long, that we retain the sense of it even when we have reduced them to the single conception which is the solution. Thus the two elements are blended according to the formula of the comic. I remember once to have seen a young man on a railroad train watching intently the time-table while he waited for the train to start. As the train moved at precisely the moment indicated by the table, he burst into a little laugh. He was apparently not much used to travel, and the blending in a single act of the two elements which seemed to him hardly congruous had upon him the effect of a joke. Of a similar nature is the laugh of pleasure. This always expresses at least a mild degree of surprise ; and the surprise shows that an event has occurred in spite of some degree of improbability. The actual happening and the improbability, great or small, are the incongruous elements that are united in our thought. "What," we exclaim, "my friend here! I hardly expected it." The smile of happiness expresses the same thing, only in a less degree. The smiling face of joy implies a certain undefined sense of the rarity of the pleasure in some aspect or other. It shows that the pleasure is not yet ranged with the commonplace.

Somewhat similar is the laugh of gratified vanity; only in this case the sense of superiority tends to raise one above one's fellows, so far as one's own feeling is concerned. One's sympathy is somewhat lessened, and one can easily see something ludicrous in what might under other circumstances cause sympathy. In the laugh of exultation over a fallen foe, enmity does more thoroughly what conceit does in the case just referred to. The conqueror has no sympathy to prevent his regarding the downfall of his enemy in a wholly ludicrous light.

With this may be associated the laugh of gayety. This may, perhaps, be best observed in the gayety of the child. The reality of life has not yet got the child fairly in its grasp. The child has had no experience by which pain and loss are easily suggested. In the case of a fall, for instance, while the man looking on might fear a broken limb, the child looking on might see only the comic aspect of the affair. A like contrast is to be noticed in regard to less serious matters. The child is always bubbling over with laughter. Every little surprise, everything that has the slightest air of incongruity, stirs its mirth. The man takes things seriously; the child has not yet reached the stage when many things are serious. What inexperience does for the child, that good spirits does for his elders. As one's spirits rise, one becomes emancipated from the bondage to things that at other times seem so real. In moments of gayety one no longer takes everything *au grand sérieux*. The thousand little incongruities, accidental or designed, that would at other times be disregarded, or regarded with impatience, now move to mirth; and the man or the woman ripples into laughter like a child.

The same point may be illustrated by the fact that words which were originally used to express only the ludicrous come, in popular speech, to stand for objects or events that might be covered by the general formula for the comic, although the height of the comic has not been reached by them, or though they may have even a tragic aspect. I once, while travelling, overheard one young woman relating to another some sad family history, in which two or three deaths had followed one another in close connection, under very similar circumstances. The response, made with the utmost solemnity was, "How funny!" In the Yankee dialect, I have heard more than once the word "ridiculous" used to express the most extreme moral condemnation. Mrs. Stowe, who is one of the best reporters of this form of speech, does not let this idiom escape her. In "The Pearl of Orr's Island," she makes Captain Kittridge exclaim, after hearing how a man in the neighborhood had tried to induce a boy to go on a piratical cruise with him, and to raise the money for it by robbery, "That ar 's rediculous conduct in Atkinson. He ought to be talked to;" and again he says: "That ar Atkinson 's too rediculous for anything."[1] This use of the

---

[1] As I have spoken of Mrs. Stowe's fidelity in reproducing New England idioms, I must protest against the "ar" in "that ar." I do not believe that this is ever heard in New England.

words "funny" and "ridiculous" illustrate the
manner in which, as we have seen, men sometimes laugh at that which is not really ludicrous,
but which might be brought under the formula
for the ludicrous ; namely, the blending of incongruous elements in one conception.

The question, why the sense of the ludicrous
should be expressed by the particular spasm
called laughter, is one that psychical physiology
has not yet satisfactorily answered. If physiol-
ogists could explain why tickling should produce
laughter, that would perhaps be an important
step in the solution of the higher question that
is before us, and I am inclined to think that here
is where the investigation should begin. So far
as I know, the matter has been taken up only at
the other end. Indeed, men often like to begin
with the most complicated examples of the object
of study. Of course the immediate interest is
greater in this method ; and there is the added
advantage to the investigator that an erroneous
solution is less easily detected.

It is always "that 'ere" and "this 'eer" for "that there" and
"this here," equivalent to *cela* and *ceci*, which happen to be good
French, while their humble American kin, of equally good ex-
traction, are regarded as vulgar. The "ar" Mrs. Stowe must
have brought from the South.

Herbert Spencer has twice attacked this problem, of which he gives two solutions, distinct yet not incompatible. One of these explains the phenomena both of tears and of laughter. I confess the explanation is somewhat ghastly. An account of dropsy and of the effect of blisters precedes the solution of the problem. The solution is this : When the brain is surcharged with blood, laughter, by checking respiration, checks the oxidation of the blood, and the incipient congestion is relieved. This may very well be ; but why my brain, that has been taxed without any ill effect, it may be all day, should be thrown into such a dangerous congestion without this relief, simply by seeing a dandy's hat blow off, is still inexplicable.

The other explanation is more ingenious and plausible, though not wholly satisfactory. It assumes that the sense of the ludicrous arises from a certain balking of our expectation. We are expecting something grand ; in its place appears something trivial. A clown runs to his horse as if to leap over him, but suddenly stops and simply pats him. We have a store of energy to meet the expected grave thought or gymnastic performance. This energy, not needed, takes

the easiest road to spend itself, and this road
is found along the laughter-causing nerves. This
implies that in anything comic the less trivial element always precedes, and the more trivial follows. Indeed, Spencer says distinctly : " Laughter naturally results only when consciousness
is unawares transferred from great things to
small, only when there is what we call a *descending* incongruity." But what shall be said of this
proposition in the face of a couplet like the following, which has caused a laugh to a good many
unreasoning persons : —

> " And like a lobster boiled, the morn
> From black to red began to turn " ?

This is certainly not a descending incongruity,
but the reverse. The comparison indeed is of
a great thing with a small, but the small comes
first ; and there is no store of accumulated and
unexpended energy to be let off.

I wish that Mr. Spencer had answered the
questions with which he opens his essay on
" The Physiology of Laughter." They are these :
" Why do we smile when a child puts on a man's
hat ? Or what induces us to laugh on reading
that the corpulent Gibbon was unable to rise
from his knees after making a tender declara-
tion ? "

I cannot see that Mr. Spencer's theory would apply to the child with the hat, except when at the first glance we think it to be a man, and then discover our mistake. When we see the child put on the hat and strut before us, there is no descending incongruity; if either, there is an ascending one : and yet this case would provoke a smile as readily as the other.

In the case of the corpulent Gibbon, Mr. Spencer's formula might seem, at first sight, to apply better. We expect to see him get up, and he does not. This is certainly not an ascending incongruity; quite otherwise! I appeal, however, to any one who has ever laughed at the incident to say whether this is the point of the story. Suppose that Gibbon had been stooping for any other purpose, trivial or grave, from picking up a pin to admiring a flower, or verifying a botanical discovery, would his inability to rise be anything like as funny? It is the association in our thought of the ideal Romeo with this awkward corpulency that is acting his part which we find so ludicrous.

The theory of laughter, as held by Kant, brings us, as I conceive, a little nearer to the facts of the case, though only a little. The sense of the ludicrous, according to Kant, arises when the mind has been strained in the expectation of something real, and finds, not the opposite of the thing that was presupposed, but absolutely nothing. Thus, to use his own example, if we are told of a man who was so frightened that every hair on his head turned white, though we do not believe it, we do not laugh ; but if we are told that the man was so frightened that every hair in his wig turned white, it is ludicrous. The mind that was intent on the story finds that the whole was a mere nothing. Had Kant possessed the advantage which Herbert Spencer enjoys, of a familiarity with the later results of physiological investigation, he might have anticipated Mr. Spencer's theory of the physiology of laughter, which would have fitted his psychological explanation perfectly. Energy is roused by one's interest in the story ; and when one finds that it has no serious meaning, this energy is dissipated, as in Spencer's statement. The difficulty is, however, that Kant takes a very limited view of the comic. He seems to find it only in the jest, as Schopenhauer practically found it only in the blunder.

If Mr. Spencer's very ingenious explanation

of laughter has any universal significance, it
must be found in the fact that the comic has to
do with the form alone, and not with the reality
of things. The more or less sudden passage in
our thought from substantial relations to merely
formal ones may, perhaps, leave a certain amount
of unemployed energy to find vent in the manner
indicated.

A difficulty may remain, however, in the fact
that the theory seems to require a certain degree
of suddenness in the apprehension of the comic.
It is, indeed, often maintained that the incongruity, if it is to excite mirth, must break upon us
suddenly. No one, it is said, ever laughs at an
old joke. Freshness certainly adds much to a
joke ; but how often we hear persons say of some
incident that it makes them laugh whenever
they think of it ! "Then your worship must not
tell the story of Ould Grouse in the gun-room,"
cried honest Diggory, when Squire Hardcastle
told the servants, whom he was training for the
unwonted occasion of guests at dinner, that if
he happened to say a good thing or tell a good
story at table, they must not all burst out
a-laughing as if they belonged to the company.
"Then, ecod, your worship must not tell the

story of Ould Grouse in the gun-room. I can't help laughing at that — he, he, he! — for the soul of me. We have laughed at that these twenty years, — ha, ha, ha!"

I am not sure that this difficulty is insurmountable. It may be that, in anticipation of the coming point of an old story, one more or less unconsciously stores up energy for the laugh at the end. This might be done by playing with one's self that the previous incidents are to be taken seriously, though one knows all the time the point up to which they are leading. We certainly do something of this kind in reading an old story that has a serious interest, a familiar play of Shakespeare, for example. We read as if we did not know what was coming, and are moved at the end as if we had never read it before. In this manner the effect of suddenness in a joke may be produced, even if the jest be an old one, and the explanation of laughter under discussion may hold good.

Kant, however, was not familiar with the later physiological investigations, and thus could not use their results in the solution of the problem before him. The explanation that he gives of laughter, on the basis of his theory of the comic, may perhaps strike us as a little singular. The mind, he says, is expecting to find something, and it finds nothing. In its surprise it looks back to see if this be really so, and discovers again that it is. This vibration or oscillation of the mind, rapidly repeated, sets the body in motion; and hence results laughter, which physical process is all that Kant recognizes as pleasurable in the sense of the comic.

Without accepting Kant's explanation of laughter, which is certainly ingenious, I am interested to notice how perfectly it would adapt itself to that part of my own statement which I have taken from Schopenhauer; better, indeed, than to Kant's own theories.

According to this, the sense of the comic arises from the attempt to bring together things that are too incongruous to be combined. The mind seizes one and tries to fit it to the other. Failing in that, it lets go the first and seizes the second, which proves equally impracticable. It flies back to the first, and this process repeats itself with inconceivable rapidity. Take, as an illustration, the conundrum, "When you are riding a donkey, what fruit do you resemble?" The answer is, of course, "A pear." Here begins the process of which I spoke. What fruit? A pear. But a donkey is not a fruit. It must mean two of us. But it can't be two of us, because the question said what fruit. And so on indefinitely. Or we go a step further. We accept the fact that the pear means two of us. But who are the two? I am one and the donkey another. No, that cannot be. The donkey is one and I am another. Worse still. Thus the process goes on. Now the mind, in this vibration which I have described, must, according to the psycho-physiological theories of Kant, which as it will be remembered I do not indorse, start a vibratory movement among certain corpuscles of the brain. This vibration becomes violent as it extends from its source. It runs down the nerves with that pleasant titillation which we all know. Becoming still more violent, it convulses the body, until at last it breaks out into the " he, he " of the fool, or the " haw, haw " of the clown.

But why need we try to explain and justify the fact of laughter? According to the principles of natural selection, is not the fact enough? According to this theory, in the innumerable changes through which life passes in its evolution, all varieties of form and action have at some moment their opportunity. If they are helpful they endure; if otherwise, they die out with their possessors. I will venture to close this discussion with an apologue which may illustrate this matter, the significance of which will, I trust, excuse the levity of its form. We may, in our thought, go back to the moment when our apelike progenitors were becoming human. The generations succeeded one another more rapidly than now; and as the earth was passing hurriedly through changes of temperature, if not of structure, each generation may be supposed to have been widely different from that which had preceded. It was a time of transition. There was an ambition such as has not since then existed upon the earth. It was a time of trial. How the foremost individuals of one generation must have differed from those of the last, or even from the less cultivated of their own. Think of the burdens of polite society! Think of Great-grandfather Ape refusing to be put into his little bed, and outraging in many ways the delicate and cultivated sensibilities of his descendants! Think of the cares of housekeeping, of servants caught wild in the forest to be initiated into the mysteries of the kitchen! No wonder that all this

proved too much for these would-be founders of
a new order of life! No wonder that they
peaked and pined in the midst of their struggles!
But suddenly there echoed a strange sound
through the wilderness. Was it a cry of pain?
It seemed so. But those features certainly wore
no look of suffering. Whenever one of those
miserable awkwardnesses of which I spoke occurred, this sound would break forth with its
strange but not unpleasing vibrations. The individual who made it seemed refreshed and exhil-
arated by what was crushing the life out of all
others. While they pined he grew fat. His
children inherited the habit which began with
him, and with it inherited his cheerful strength;
and thus, while other families dwindled and
passed away, the descendants of the man who
laughed alone endured, to form the race of man
that laughs.

III. DUTY.

THE ULTIMATE FACTS OF ETHICS.

THE moral law stands among the manifold relations of the world, apparently as the great exception. In other matters we do not hesitate to trace the connection of finite cause and effect. In regard to duty, our natural impulse is to recognize the presence of some higher element. In practical matters, we ordinarily seek that which is most advantageous to ourselves. In the presence of duty, this personal advantage is neglected. Thus the moral law rises above all the entanglements of our thought and our life. It is not strange that Kant felt that here we are in contact with the absolute reality; that, while everywhere else we are in the world of phenomena, in the moral law we touch the substance of things. It is not strange that this fact, so impressive and so exceptional, should stimulate the investigating spirit of our time; that our scientific explorers should bring their scaling ladders and seek to climb this awful height, in order that they may plant there, also, the flag of the all-conquering science.

We are all sufficiently the children of our age to sympathize with this attempt. We must notice, however, one point in which the investigation into the nature of the moral law is distinguished from inquiries in regard to other matters of scientific research. In this we must test our results by their consequences. The moral law is one of the fundamental facts of our experience ; and the object of the questioner is to explain this, not to disturb it. If the conclusions to which he comes are such as to weaken and confuse the moral sense, the very conditions of the inquiry are violated. In other words, if our analysis is correct, it must be confirmed by our synthesis. This assumption is not merely a practical one. It is a case in which the practical and the theoretical coincide. The moral sense is one of the ultimate factors of our nature. The love of the right and the love of the true share the sovereignty of our souls. Neither can dethrone the other. If the pursuit of truth seem to weaken the moral sense, it shows that the pursuit has been following the wrong trail. This position may seem unscientific and archaic. It is so, tried before the bar of science alone. Before the high court of ultimate appeal, however, in which Reason sits as judge, it is enforced. Here no one faculty of the nature is permitted to do violence to any other. This position does not justify us in assuming a theory to be true simply because it would give new sanctions to the moral law. It does justify us in rejecting as insufficient any explanation of the moral impulse that would weaken its authority.

A superficial view of the facts of the moral consciousness may easily give rise to false and harmful theories. Such a superficial view naturally suggests the idea of a fluctuating and changeful morality, and may thus seem to leave no place for any firm and enduring basis of moral relations. Indeed, when we remember what different things are considered right by different peoples and at different times, it seems almost hopeless that any order should be introduced into the chaos. We are tempted to think that there is no right and no morality. The Fijian thinks it his duty to put his parents to death even while they are hardly weakened by age. In ordinary

times, we are told not to lie, not to steal, and
not to kill; but, so soon as war breaks out, all
our familiar maxims seem to count for nothing.
Men feel it their duty to kill, to steal, and to cir-
cumvent. If such facts do not prove to us that
there is no such thing as a permanent moral
principle in man, they must at least affect our
conception of this. It is obvious that the moral
sense cannot be regarded as containing within
itself the requirement to perform certain specific
duties. There is no table of commandments
written upon the heart. Either duty, or what
we regard as such, is indeed the outgrowth of
circumstances, and varies with time, place, and
condition ; or else it is something which lies behind all definite rules and simply takes form in
these. It is elastic, not as yielding to pressure,
affirming itself with more or less power according to the difficulty or the peril; but elastic in
the sense that, while it remains the same, its
method of asserting itself varies according to the
circumstances to which it is to be applied.

Of course it would be easy to say that all variation like that to which I have referred is the
result merely of an imperfect development of the
moral sense, and to urge that, if the moral sense

were equally developed in all, the same standard of duty would be accepted by all. Such an explanation might apply to some cases of divergence, but it would leave many not accounted for.

If there is such a thing as a uniform principle of ethics, then a savage, doing what he considers to be right, must be actuated by motives similar to those which actuate us when we do what we regard as right, even though from our standpoint we consider what he does as in itself wrong, and though he from his standpoint should condemn us.

Many factors have united in the development of our moral nature, which cannot be regarded as its source. Natural selection has doubtless played its part; education has had its share in the work. But natural selection must have had something with which to start; and education develops faculties which it could not create. There must be certain ultimate principles which give to morality its special quality. It is these which we are to seek.

It may be well, before entering upon our search, to ask what it is precisely which we may hope to find. Can we hope to discover some principle which may serve in any given case as a

test to determine what course of action is wrong
and what is right? In regard to certain strongly
marked contrasts, perhaps this might be accomplished. For the most of life, however, I think
that this would be hoping too much. In the
discussion of the elements of tragedy, we have
had really placed before us, under another name,
the sphere in which duty exists. We have seen
that there is nothing wrong in itself. There is
no primary instinct or impulse of the nature
which is not, in itself considered, good. The
pleasure that is in some cases taken in the
suffering of others has caused difficulty to some
students of ethics. This pleasure, however, I
conceive to be, not primary in the nature, but
secondary. If all the natural impulses are right,
the only wrong is found in yielding to one under
circumstances in which we should have yielded
to another We might hope, then, to be able to
arrange the various primary impulses in a hier-
archy, according to which the lower should always be subject to the higher. We should thus
have a mechanical device which would settle
every case as it might arise. In fact, however,
the question of degree is as important as that
of precedence. Common sense and conscience

must still be left to settle the matter between themselves. It is as impossible to give definite rules for the perfect life as it is to give definite rules in accordance with which a beautiful poem or painting shall certainly be produced. We have a right to expect, however, that a knowledge of the true principles upon which morality rests should strengthen the moral sense, and make it easier to obey the voice of duty. If it helps the decision in any difficult case, it will be because it thus quickens the moral insight, rather than because it furnishes any hard-and-fast system of rules.

In approaching our theme, two questions should be distinguished which are often confounded. One of these questions is, What is the impulse by which men perform the acts which we call right? The second question is, What is the nature of the sense of duty by which men feel an obligation to perform such acts? The neglect to notice the distinction implied by these questions has done much to confuse the study of ethics. Acts that we know as right must have long been performed, and must have received a certain recognition, before the tendency to perform them was reinforced by the sense of obligation. In fact, the sense of duty would seem to be a comparatively late development of human nature, and it is only an occasional element in the ethical development of man. It may further be said that, while the sense of duty implies a comparatively high development of the spirit, yet its presence also implies a certain difficulty in right doing. It shows a lack of freedom and spontaneity in the direction of the right. A man who performs a righteous act from a sense of duty stands much higher than one who does not perform it at all; but one who performs it because it seems the most natural thing in the world, simply because he wants to, stands still higher. If the sense of duty involves such imperfection, we may naturally ask, Whence comes our reverence for it? This reverence is justified by the fact that the feeling of duty really implies an advance in right doing. It implies an invasion of realms not yet wholly subjugated, and therefore held with some difficulty.

All that I would now insist upon is that we have two questions instead of one. They are, indeed, closely connected; and the 'answer to one will throw light upon the other. They demand, however, separate treatment.

We must first ask, Why do men tend to perform certain acts that we call right? and then
ask, Whence comes, when it does come, the
sense of obligation? The answer to the first
question will be purely psychological. The answer to the second will involve elements that are
metaphysical.

Our first question is, then, as to the nature of
the impulse to perform right actions.

Before proceeding to the positive answer to
the question before us, it will be well to notice a
widespread error in regard to the matter. This
is the assumption that the first impulse to moral
activity was furnished by religion. This assumption is sometimes made in the interest of religion, since it recognizes this as the basis of the
moral life. Sometimes it is made in the interest
of a scientific explanation of the facts of morality,
since the influence of superstition is a recognized
force, that may be easily regarded as applied in
this direction. In either case, the assumption is
without foundation.

If anything is certain in regard to the lowest
forms of religion, it is that either they are without any moral significance, or that they possess
this in a very small degree. The favor of the

supernatural beings is not to be won by virtue, but by offerings and prayers. So far as a future life is recognized, there seems to be little if any difference in the state of those who have been good and those who have been evil; if, indeed, the terms good and evil have, at this stage of human development, any meaning. So far as any difference is supposed to exist in regard to the state of spirits after death, it depends upon some merely ritualistic matter. Among the Tahitians, we are told that only the neglect of some rite or ceremony is visited by the displeasure of the deities in another world. "I never could learn," says Ellis, "that they expected in the world of spirits any difference in the treatment of a kind, generous, peaceful man and that of a cruel, parsimonious, and quarrelsome one." And Cook says that the Otaheitans do not suppose that their actions here in the least affect their future state, or, indeed, that they come under the cognizance of their deities at all. If anything besides the fitting service to the gods determines the condition of the spirit in the future life, it is, in general, something that has as little moral significance as such service. Thus the Fijians believe that women not tatooed would

have a hard time in the next world. Men who
had not slain any enemy would be compelled to
beat dirt with a club. Bachelors had a particu-
larly hard time getting to the Fijian paradise.
Their spirits were liable to be seized by one of
the gods, and killed by smashing against a stone.[1]

Not only did the gods not especially favor the
good, they often favored what we should consider
evil. Among the Fijians, cruelty, murder, can-
nibalism, treachery, and revenge, we are told,
were sanctioned by the gods. This is evidently
a degradation of religion, falling below the zero
point of ethical indifference, as a more fully developed religion rises above it. It shows, however, religion to be affected by the ethical ideas
of a people rather than affecting them. It inten-
sifies these feelings, whatever they may be.
Through his religion, the ambition of a Fijian to
be a murderer was increased ; but it was the ambition itself, common among the people, which
procured for it the divine sanction.

This relation of religion to morality is illustrated even among the more developed religions.
Among the Vedic hymns there is some evidence

---

[1] These examples, and others that will be given, are taken
from the *Descriptive Sociology*, compiled under the direction of
Herbert Spencer, a most admirable and useful work.

of an ethical content of the religion. Varuna represented more than any other divinity the moral idea. Ritual is, however, in general, far more obvious than sanctions of morality. In the Mazdean religion, which was perhaps the most ethical of the older religions, moral and ceremonial injunctions are dwelt upon with equal force. In the Hebrew religion, the ceremonial law holds a prominent position. Even in the ten commandments, the injunction to keep the Sabbath is placed among those which insist upon love to God and righteousness towards man. In the teaching of Jesus, righteousness and religion are found each interpenetrated by the other. There is no religion apart from righteousness, and no righteousness not sanctioned by religion. This high position religion, however, could not long maintain. The popular belief, even of the present day, while insisting upon a righteous life, makes certain spiritual exercises which have little connection with this of hardly less importance; and beliefs, together with such exercises, are supposed to have much to do with the condition of the spirit in the life after death. In the Catholic Church, certain forms and ceremonies are still believed to be essential to salvation.

By the side of this indifference of religion to morality among the lower peoples, we find the beginnings, and sometimes beautiful manifestations, of the moral sentiments. These peoples are, indeed, in a state of innocence. Apparently with little sense of right or wrong as such, the natural impulses of the heart, whether right or wrong, freely manifest themselves.[1] Sometimes we are shocked by cruelty and sensuality, sometimes charmed by the manifestation of the most beautiful traits of human character. The Malagasy, we read, treat one another with more humanity than we do. There no one is miserable, if it is in the power of his neighbors to help him. There is love, tenderness, and generosity which might shame us, and moral honesty, too. In the Congo markets, we are told, every transaction is conducted with truthfulness and confidence. There is no deceit practised, — not because it is

---

[1] It is a state of things that is in part covered by Ovid's description of the Golden Age : —

> "Quæ vindice nullo
> Sponte sua, sine lege, fidem rectumque colebat.
> Pœna metusque aberant."

Only we must remember that men also did wrong without fear of punishment, and without any sense of wrong-doing.

forbidden, but because honorable dealing has become habitual.

I have not meant to picture an idyllic state, in
which the children of nature lead simple, affec-
tionate lives. The savage has terrible vices and
crimes, or what would be crimes if there were as
yet any law that should justify the term. I wish
simply to recognize the fact that in the life that
is the least developed we find, side by side, the
elements, the warfare between which forms the
plot of that great epic which we call history.,
We find the virtues existing uncommanded, and
vice and wrong existing unforbidden. As yet, so
far as these matters are concerned, there is only
a certain habit or custom which, by a control
that is to a great degree unfelt because it works
through individuals as well as upon them, shapes
the lives of men. This custom which controls is
itself a product, and cannot be used to explain
that out of which it sprang.

We are now ready to ask more directly from
what part of our nature comes the impulse to
those actions to which later we give the name
of right. The first which I shall name is so obvious that it might hardly seem worth the naming, but it is so fundamental that to omit it

would be to omit that which is most essential in the discussion. I mean the altruistic feelings, to which the names "sympathy" or "love" can be applied according to the intensity of the emotion which we would describe. We find in the most undeveloped man something of that feeling for his fellows which prompts to kind and helpful acts. We find something of this even among the lower animals. There is the self-forgetful care of the mother for her young. There is the willingness of the mother to meet suffering and death for her young. Darwin tells of a young ape that sprang to the help of his keeper who was attacked by a baboon, and that suffered wounds in the unselfish strife. All this we may be told has no moral quality whatever. It is "mere instinct." When it is said that the mother's love, for instance, is mere instinct, many feel that we have given it a pretty low place among the activities and impulses of life. We must remember, however, that what is done from instinct is done without doubt or hesitation ; while what is done from a sense of duty alone is marked by some degree of both. From this point of view, what is done from the instinct of love may perhaps seem no less admirable than that which is done from the so-called higher motive. At the stage which we are at present considering, all that concerns us is the obvious fact that in sympathy or love we have the source of the original impulse to perform many of those acts which become later recognized as right.

A slight examination will show under what various forms this principle of love will manifest itself. There is no single act which it prescribes. Its expression will vary with the circumstances of every case, and yet more with the comprehension of these circumstances. It will have to learn from experience what acts are helpful and what are injurious to others. From one's own experience one learns what is pleasant and what is painful; and love will be prompt to produce the pleasant and to diminish or to destroy the painful, so far as others are concerned. Where experience cannot reach, the result is helped out by theories and beliefs. An extreme example is of the Fijian, of whom I have already spoken, who thought it proper and right to put his parents to death. From his point of view this was an act of love. He believed that the bodily state in which one dies will be that in which he enters upon the life after death. One

who dies weak and shrivelled with age will, in
the life after death, still "drag out a ridiculous
age ;" and so he put his parents to death while
they were in full bodily and mental vigor. They,
on their part, took the same view, and were glad
to have the act accomplished. A highly educated
Chinese mandarin, who was for a time connected
with Harvard University as a teacher, aroused
the indignation of persons who had received possibly exaggerated accounts of the suffering that
he was causing to his young daughter by subject-
ing her feet to the pressure practised in China in
such cases. He explained, however, that it was
an act of kindness. The real cruelty would be
to let her go back to China without this com-
pression. If her feet had been left to grow to
their natural size, she would have no status in
the society to which she naturally belonged.

There are among the savages terrible acts of a
cruel selfishness. There is a superstition no less
cruel. I am merely indicating the fact that
there are circumstances in which love will do
what may seem to be the work of selfishness or
hate.

While a regard for others would, under ordinary circumstances, lead to the preservation of

their lives and property, there may come times when a regard for the common well-being would lead to the taking of the lives and property of others. This is the case in regard to those who have committed crimes against their fellows. So in war, the regard for those with whom one is associated, or for the absolute good of the whole, may lead to the disregard of the happiness and even of the lives of others.

I have wished merely to illustrate the fact that from one central principle may spring acts that are utterly divergent; that there may be an absolute morality which does not consist in a fixed set of rules, but which manifests itself in the attempt to reach, by whatever way may seem the best, a single result.

All this that I have said about sympathy or love has been, in one way or another, often said before. This principle has been made the basis of systems of morality. It was the one principle recognized by Hume, the father of our modern utilitarianism. It is, indeed, the principle of all forms of utilitarianism. The fault of many such systems consists in the fact that they recognize this principle alone. It must be regarded as one of the ultimate facts in ethics.

It is, however, only one of these facts. There is a class of actions, of fundamental importance so far as the science of ethics is concerned, which the altruistic principle does not account for. I refer to the impulse to truthfulness, honesty, and kindred virtues. These sometimes may spring from the impulse of sympathy, but in many cases they do not. An extreme illustration of their independence of any sense of sympathy may be found in such a case as the following. A poor man owes a sum of money to a rich neighbor. The sum is large for him, but to his neighbor it would be wholly unimportant. We may suppose, further, that his neighbor has forgotten the debt, and that no one else knows of its existence. Why does this man feel moved to pay the debt? We have, as before, to consider merely what is taking place in his own mind. It is not through sympathy that he is moved; for the creditor, after he has received the money, will be practically no better off than he was before. It is not from any regard to the injury to public faith which his failure to pay the debt would involve; for, according to our supposition, no one but himself would know anything of the matter. The promise is fulfilled from a regard to himself alone. He feels that it would be unworthy of him to break the promise which he has made.

The formalities of our custom-house may give a yet more striking example. Not only is the duty that is paid by each individual traveller an inappreciable drop in the ocean of the country's revenues; so far as it may count, it is an injury. The country suffers from an excess of revenue. The traveller may believe the whole system to be a mistake and an evil. How important is the place filled by utilitarian considerations is shown by the laxity, under these circumstances, of many persons whose consciences are strict under all others, so that "custom-house oaths" have become a by-word. That these considerations do not make up the whole of morality is obvious from the openness and honesty of many under these exceptional conditions.

We must admit the importance of such examples of honesty and truthfulness to the public order. We must admit that, if the principle of truthfulness should become decayed in a single case, the chances are that it would become decayed in many cases. Individual men and women are like the piles that uphold some solid structure; the only safety is that each shall remain sound throughout. While this must be admitted, it remains none the less true that the consideration of the general welfare is not that which prompts the act of honesty or truthfulness in any given case.

We have, then, to associate with the principle of sympathy another principle, which shall hold equal rank with it. This principle we have now to seek. If, without reference to any theory, we should state in the most common language what the principle is which controls the actions in such cases as I have supposed, we should say that it is honor. The terms "altruism" and "honor" stand, however, in no organic relation to one another. They in no sense complement one another, as we should suppose the terms that express the ultimate principles of ethics would do. This leads us to suspect that the idea of honor may be reduced to a more fundamental form. In fact the method of this reduction is obvious. When a man acts from motives of honor, he acts with some reference to himself. He acts as he does because he would be ashamed to act otherwise. Thus, while acts done from an altruistic impulse have reference to others, those done from a sense of honor have a certain reference to one's self. In other words, sympathy is a principle of self-surrender, honor is one of self-assertion. The two would seem, at the first glance, not merely antithetical, but mutually exclusive. Yet they together form the two foundation principles of our moral life.

Honor has not always an ethical significance. It may sometimes be even immoral. It is possible, however, to draw a line of sharp distinction between the two kinds of honor, so as to leave no confusion between the ethical and the unethical.

A man may assert himself merely as one individual against another. He may have regard merely to his own personality. He may seek fame and power. He may seek to exalt himself at the expense of others. He may be zealous for the defence of his good name. In all this he may be wrong or he may be right. Certainly a man is justified in caring for his good name, so far as he takes no unfitting steps to accomplish this. A man has a right to regard his own dignity and not to suffer himself to be insulted. Whether in this he be right or wrong, certainly what he does in such regards has, in general, no ethical worth. A man may have a right to do things which no duty would demand. We respect a man who within proper limits maintains his rights, but we do not for this ascribe to him the praise of virtue. Such self-assertion is merely *formal.* The form of personality is maintained without regard to the content of the personality. The man regards himself merely as an individual, without regard to that which makes the substance of his nature. From this point of view all individuals are alike. They have merely a numerical value. The saint and the sinner, the savage and the man of culture, each maintains himself in his position, each tries to exalt himself, each tries at least to ward off all undue aggression and to protect himself from insult and wrong.

Although, from the point of view of pure individuality, all individuals have equal value, yet this is not the case, so far as their own estimation is concerned. Each tends to regard himself as of special importance. In some this principle of self-exaltation is very marked. They are peculiarly susceptible to what they consider slights, are peculiarly inclined to maintain some exaltation that they feel is their proper due.

The high spirit that is thus manifested adds, sometimes, a certain grace and brilliancy to the life. To this is owing, in part, the charm of the days of chivalry. The one great end of life to the knight was to make and to keep himself peerless. No shade of dishonor could rest upon him. No hint of shame could be for a moment endured. We feel the fascination of this frank and fearless heroism, even while we recognize the fact that it does not represent the highest type of life. We admit that from it has grown in part that recognition of the individual as such which marks our later civilization. We see its relationship to Christianity, which attaches infinite worth to the individual. While the sense of personal honor was so prominent in chivalry, we cannot fail to see in it, also, traces of that higher honor of which we shall later speak.

I have said that the sense of honor, regarded as merely formal self-assertion, is without ethical value. This is true of it, considered directly and in itself alone. Considered as a factor in society, it is, within due bounds, hardly less important than the altruistic feelings themselves. Though ethically worthless in itself, it is indirectly the occasion of results that are important

even from an ethical point of view. The merely
formal self-assertion stands in the same relation
to the altruistic impulses, in which the force of
repulsion stands to that of attraction in the physical world. The world could not exist if either
of these elements were absent. Just as little
could society exist if all men were wholly altruistic. While neither of these forces could be
spared, we might almost fancy that a society
which should be united by the bonds of self-interest alone would hold together better than one
from which self-interest should be wholly excluded. It is self-interest that makes the person.
It is the altruistic sentiments that make him a
person worthy of love and reverence. A man
must have relations towards himself before he
can have relations towards another. If every
man rejoiced merely in his neighbor's joy, what
real, original joy would there be for any one to
rejoice over?

The formal self-assertion and the altruistic impulses, taken together, give rise to the sense of
justice and the demand for it. If one's altruistic
feelings were perfect, one would wish that all
men should be alike favored. One would feel the
privation of another somewhat as if it were his

own. Just as, in regard to his own body, a man's natural impulse leads him to seek that all the members should be protected against the cold, each according to its special need, so in the body politic each would be guided by a like instinctive feeling to strive that all its members should be made alike happy, and should become developed each according to his own nature. This, however, would be simply universal benevolence. It would not yet be the demand for universal justice. This demand is suggested by the coöperation of the formal or individual sense of honor with the altruistic sentiments. A man resents any encroachment of others upon himself. Still more does a man of honor resent an insult or an indignity. If a man have a thoroughly sympathetic feeling towards his fellows, he will extend this sense of honor so as to cover them. He will feel any attack upon them, any indignity that is offered to them, or any encroachment upon the circle of what naturally pertains to each of them, as if it were directed against himself. He will resent the wrongs of others as if they were his own. It is this sense of resentment, felt first in what concerns one's self, and extended later to include that which concerns others, that, in coöp-

cration with the strictly altrustic feelings, gives
rise to the sense of justice.   Benevolence seeks
to make common whatever appears to it to be
the best good ; justice represses wrong.   Benevolence gives; justice recognizes and defends
rights.

It is, however, when a man in his self-assertion
has regard, not merely to the form of his self-
hood, but to its content, that direct ethical value
becomes possible. · We may find an example of
this in the ethical significance which the phrase
"*noblesse oblige*" has assumed.   It is related of
Winthrop the novelist, that the thought of his
ancestry was a constant incentive to noble acts.
He felt that he represented a line that had done
honorable work in the world.   There is a family
pride that would lead one to display or to seek
position and dignity.   When he thought of his
family, it was not merely as a family that he
thought of it.   He thought of it as a family of
solid worth and public-spirited usefulness.   When
he asserted himself, it was as a member of
such a family as this.   He asserted himself by
such acts of nobility and usefulness as he felt
were prompted by his very blood.   This is what
I mean by speaking of a self-assertion which is

not merely formal, but which involves a content. The one type of family pride would seek to exalt the family as a family. The other would seek to manifest the noble qualities which the family might be believed to have possessed.

No man stands alone in the world. Each is a member of a great society. If one asserts himself as a mere individual, he fails to assert himself as a member of the great body to which he belongs. Take, for instance, a member of a household. Such a person may assert himself, seeking to get all the comfort and good he can in perfect disregard of the rest. In that case, he asserts his formal individuality. If, however, he asserts himself as a member of this little organism, then he will be thoughtful and kind, subordinating his good to the good of those who stand in a like relation with himself.

Self-assertion will thus vary according to the content of each individuality. One person may feel himself in a special manner the member of a family, another may feel himself the member of a nation, another may feel himself a part of universal humanity.

What I wish to insist upon is, that in all these examples we have various aspects of self-asser-

tion. The loving and helpful man asserts himself as truly as the hard and selfish man. The
difference between the two is to be found in the
content of the self which each affirms. A cheap
bit of cynicism is sometimes displayed in an
assertion based upon the fact that the good man
likes to do good just as the bad man likes to do
evil. All men, it is said, are alike selfish; for
each does what pleases him best. The distinction that has just been made shows the fallacy of
this reasoning. Each is alike selfish, if we care
to use the word in this connection, so far as the
affirmation of the self is concerned. They differ
in the self that is thus affirmed. The self of the
one, being bound up in his own petty individuality, is hardly more than a point; the self of the
other broadens and includes the lives about him.
It is not to the act of self-assertion, it is to the
self which is asserted, that we give our praise or
blame.

To this self-assertion I have given the name
of honor. The rightfulness of this name may
easily be shown. It is obvious in the case of
the merely formal self-assertion in which a man
insists upon recognition or repels an insult. The
use of the term "honor" is less fitting where the

self that is affirmed consists merely of the passions and greeds of the nature. It becomes fitting again in regard to that larger content of self of which I have spoken. A man who is conscious that he is not a merely abstract being, standing in and for himself; who feels that in the fibres of his life are intertwined the fibres of other lives, so that in affirming himself he affirms these larger relations, and in affirming these he affirms himself, — such a man feels that to fail in any act of kindness and helpfulness would be foreign to his nature. It would be beneath him. His sense of honor forbids him to stoop to anything selfish, petty, or mean.

It may be thought that in using the words "unworthy" and "beneath" we have introduced ethical conceptions foreign to the facts upon which our analysis has been based. Why, from the point of view of mere self-assertion, should the idea of worthiness be introduced? Why should not a man feel simply that an emotion or an act is foreign to him? Whence comes the thought that it is beneath him, so that by stooping to it he would feel himself dishonored? The sense of honor or of dishonor in these relations comes from the recognition of the greater or less fulness of the life. The feeling is based upon a quantitative difference. The rich man who becomes suddenly poor, the man of public or princely stand who becomes suddenly reduced to a position of mediocrity, may have a sense of mortification. This results from the fact that they find their lives so circumscribed in comparison to their former experience. Before, their influence, their control, their recognition, had extended far. Their lives had each a thousand tributaries. Now, each life stands in the narrowness of its petty self. In like manner, the opulent or royal soul, that has felt itself to be one with the great human life about it, would feel itself narrowed and thus dishonored by any act through which it should cut itself off from these larger relations. In this sense it is that we may speak of stooping to a selfish act, or may say that such an act is not only foreign to the nature, but is unworthy of it and beneath it. We are apt to speak of the wickedness of sin. I am not sure that it would not be as true and more effective if we should speak oftener of the meanness of it.

We have thus far considered illustrations of honor, in the ethical use of that word, which involve actions of the same sort as those which are prompted by sympathy or love. In such cases, this latter principle is, in general, the moving power. Men perform these altruistic acts from altruistic motives. The sense of honor, as we have described it, hardly makes itself felt. In cases, however, where the altruistic feeling may not be quite strong enough to produce a result, the feeling of honor may come to its support. A man may hesitate to take the trouble or to bear the burden that is required to meet some rightful demand upon his time or strength. Then, suddenly, he may think that he should be ashamed of himself if he failed; and the pride of self-assertion may accomplish that to which sympathy alone was not quite equal.

There are, however, cases in which the sense of honor stands alone. It was, indeed, such as these that first made us feel the need of complementing the altruistic feelings by this additional motive. I refer to the impulse to truthfulness and honesty, when these might cost the actor dear, and would really benefit no one else. In regard to such instances, we are in the habit of using the term "honor." A business man who will not stoop to fraud, a man whose word may be accepted as confidently as another man's bond, — these we call honorable men. They have a sense of honor which controls their lives. We have then to ask, How does this use of the word " honor " agree with our former use of it? In what sense is the honor of integrity equivalent to self-assertion? The answer is obvious. A man of honor feels that his spoken word is a part of himself. This stubbornness of self-assertion must not be confounded with the self-assertion with which a man may obstinately persist in his own course, or in the accomplishment of certain ends which he has set before himself, or the disappointment with which he sees the failure of his plans. The feeling of a man at the thought of breaking his word is not that of a general at the thought of being driven back from a position that he has taken. A man's plans, his success and failures in the world, the riches that he may gain or lose, — these are all outside of himself. He may be mortified that he has not had wisdom or strength to carry out his purposes, that he has been outwitted or overpowered. All this, however, is not akin to the shame which one feels at the thought of a broken word; for the promise was a part of himself, and, when he is false to it, he is false to himself.

Another aspect of the case is even more important. Truthfulness is the solidity of the social structure. We have seen that the undetected falsehood of the individual would not affect this. The man of honor is, however, ashamed to grant himself a laxity that he denies to others. In affirming himself as a member of the social order, he affirms all the obligations which rest upon the members of this order.

What has been said of truthfulness has been with special reference to the keeping of promises. The considerations adduced apply with less force to the speaking of truth in regard to past or present facts. It is very natural, therefore, to find that men are often very strict in fulfilling engagements, and in recognizing the rights of property, who are very lax so far as truth-speaking in general is concerned. Falsehood, however, involves a granting to one's self an indulgence that one would hesitate to grant freely to all the world. In case one would grant the indulgence to all the world, as indeed we do in regard to many minor matters, the sense of honor is not aroused in the matter. Our business here is not to settle cases of casuistry, but simply to show that the sense of honor, and the truthful-

ness that results from this, stand in direct relation to the demands which we make upon others.

In connection with the sense of honor as manifested in honesty and truthfulness, we may consider it in reference to the vices that degrade a
man.   One who takes a true view of himself
sees the various elements of his nature to exist
in certain relations of superiority and subordination.   He sees that he is really himself, really
a man, so long as this relation is maintained.
If the body assumes supremacy over the spirit,
if the passions control the reason, the proper
subordination is lost.   The man is no longer
himself.   He no longer asserts himself.   He is
not a man, for he has assimilated himself to the
beast.   This degradation his sense of honor forbids.

The sense of honor, as I have thus described
it, belongs to a comparatively late period of development.   In its earliest form it is as simple
and unconscious as is the altruistic sentiment.
One keeps his word, for instance, as naturally as
one performs an act of kindness.   The savage
would seem to have no more shame at a lie than
at an act of cruelty.   Yet he may at times keep
his word at some cost to himself, just as he may

at times do an act of kindness at some cost to himself. It is this honesty that later becomes developed into the sense of honor, just as it is this more or less occasional kindness which later becomes developed into the altruistic sentiment. Both originated independently of law or religion and independently also of that custom or public sentiment for which they furnish the basis.

If this incipient altruism and this incipient sense of honor are natural to man, why, it may be asked, do they not manifest themselves more uniformly and more persistently? To this it must be answered that, though they are natural, yet they do not constitute man's whole nature. With this altruism and this honor, in the highest sense of the term, is associated the formal sense of honor, or, at this lowest stage of development, the formal self-assertion. From the necessities of the case, this develops earlier than the others; and it may often be found in collision with them. The instinct of self-preservation in its simplest form, — the instinct, that is, of preserving one's self as an individual, that instinct which man shares with the brute, and even with the plant and the rock, — this is the root upon which the existence of the individual and the race depends.

It is long before this instinct of self-preservation attaches itself to the content rather than to the form of the life. Perhaps we should say, rather, that the content which it first embraces is the comfort and pleasure of life. Of these the altruistic feelings and the higher sense of honor would often demand the sacrifice. It is not strange, therefore, that the manifestation of them should be intermittent.

We have considered the psychological elements that prompt to the actions which we recognize to be right. We have as yet not faced the question, Whence comes the sense of obligation to do the right, and whence comes the reproach of conscience when we have done wrong? This, it will be remembered, was the second question to which we proposed to seek an answer.

If, for instance, we consider the altruistic sentiments, the thought of the suffering of another may give us pain. This is sufficiently accounted for by the fact of sympathy, but sympathy does not explain to us whence come the special pain and self-reproach when we think that we caused the suffering. It explains the shock which the sight of death might give us; it does not explain the horror of a murderer's remorse. So, too, we may understand why, other things being equal, one should speak the truth rather than tell a lie. We see no reason for the condemnation with which one visits himself for an act of dishonesty. Unquestionably, external influences have had much to do with developing this sense of obligation. What one has been taught from one's childhood to do, what one's race has been taught through countless generations to do, it is easy to see would tend to produce something like the sense of obligation. Especially would this be the case when such teaching had been reinforced by the sanctions of religion and by legal enactment. It is difficult to disentangle these influences from others that may have coöperated with these. The sense of duty is, however, qualitatively unlike all other impulses. Men are trained also, and the generations of men are trained, in other ways and to other results. These results cannot be confounded with the moral sense. The maxims of prudence have been urged side by side with those of justice and benevolence; but a man who violates the one calls himself a fool, while one who violates the other reproaches himself with wrong-doing. The pain that comes from the violation of the customs of society may be as sharp as a pang of conscicnce. It can, however, never be confounded with this.

From the nature of the sense of obligation and of conscience, we should expect, further, that they should stand in some direct relation to the original impulse to which they give sanction. The reproach of conscience which adds to this impulse the authority of a law must in some way be the result of this impulse. The condemnation is that one did not yield to this impulse. It is thus, as we might say, the rejected impulse itself that turns back upon him who neglected it, and utters its reproach. It thus reveals itsclf in its deeper and truer nature. What seemed a mere impulse among other impulses is found to have its root deep in the nature of the spirit, perhaps even to penetrate through this, to pass beyond the individual, and to become one with thc root by which he himself is bound to that larger life of which he is a part.

It is interesting to notice in this connection that often the sense of obligation does not make itself felt until the wrong act has been committed. Indeed, it is probable that in general the power of the law of duty is first felt through its penalties ; that the verdict, This oughtest thou to have done, or This oughtest thou to have left undone, is heard before the command, This shalt thou do, or This shalt thou leave undone. It is in the light of an offended conscience that one first reads the commandments of the law. Fichte maintains that such was the nature of the development of the moral sense. Men learned what was right through the inner condemnation which they experienced when they had done what is wrong. After each experience of this kind, the memory of the condemnation became the utterance of the law. This moral development is an advance along the line of least resistance. It is found that conscience interposes its barrier as soon as men wander into any course but one. Thus a boy thoughtlessly throws a stone at a bird and kills it. In many cases of the kind, the boy is indifferent as to the result. In others, so soon as he holds the dead body of the bird in his hand, his joy is changed to horror and re-morse. He has learned a lesson for a lifetime. A striking exemplification of the same process is found in Browning's poems, entitled " Before " and " After."

This does not mean that one must commit all the sins in the Decalogue in order to realize their sinfulness. A single example may have a multitude of applications. One may learn the lesson through condemnation of another, as well as through condemnation of one's self. The results of the experience of the past are in some sense inherited ; while imagination may, in some degree, replace the actual experiment.

In seeking the simplest form which the sense of obligation may assume, we need then to look more carefully at the elements of love and honor which we have already recognized. Love seems to us so natural a thing that we often fail to see the real mystery of it. A man seems shut up in himself. He has his pains and his pleasures, his hopes and his fears. Suddenly, we find him moved by the pains and pleasures of another more than by his own, filled with an anxiety for another greater than the care with which he regards himself. This phenomenon is sometimes explained by the fact of what may be called imitativeness. When one sees another suffering from a wound, one has an incipient feeling of pain, as if one were suffering from a like wound. Thus, by a kind of reflection, we take the joys and the sorrows of another life into our own. This fact does not, however, explain that power of sympathy by which we suffer not only with another, but for him. It might explain why we should hate a sufferer the sight of whom brings us pain ; it does not show why we should love him. There are indeed persons who do feel a certain anger towards the unfortunate. Miss Cobbe gives an example of this kind in the story of a child who fell, I think, from a bed, and burst into loud crying at the pain which resulted from the fall. Another child flew at it angrily, and began to beat it. Such sympathy as has been described may lead to attempts to relieve others because thereby one relieves himself. That strange metamorphosis, however, in which another's pain becomes our own, and our own sorrow is that of another, in which we lose all consciousness of ourselves, and feel only the gladness or the grief of another, — all this mere imitative sympathy cannot explain.

The truth is that no one of us is merely an individual. The altruistic feelings are as natural as the selfish feelings, even if they are in most cases less strong. I have called this stretching of our life beyond ourselves, this setting of the

centre of our life in another, a mystery. It is so
merely from the point of view of our individual-
istic and atomistic theories of life. It is no mystery to the heart itself, which finds in it only its
natural existence. It is no mystery to a more
profound philosophy, to which the words " mere
individual " have no meaning. There is no mere
individual, any more than there is a mere leaf on
a tree. We are the manifestations of a life larger
than that of any individual, a life that lives in
the lives about us, so that we may feel, in a certain sense and to a certain degree, one with them
as with it. In this fact we find, as I conceive, a
source of the sense of obligation and of the condemning power of conscience.

Conscience implies something broader and
larger than our individual lives. In the sense of
obligation, we feel the presence and the power of
this larger reality. This presence and power,
which give their peculiar significance to the
sense of duty, are often regarded as implying by
necessity a recognition of God. This, doubtless,
is in some sense implied in the facts under consideration ; but it is, I conceive, a mistake to
affirm that duty and conscience necessarily imply a conscious recognition of the divine pres-

ence. They do not imply the conscious recognition of any metaphysical or theological principle. They imply simply that *the life of the spirit is weighted by something vaster than itself*, something in which it is somehow bound up, but from which, in wrong-doing, it has in a sense separated itself. This vaster somewhat I conceive to be, in its simplest form, that common life of which the life of each is partaker. One is drawn into harmony with that, somewhat as the world, by the power of attraction, is drawn into harmony with the other worlds which in connection with it makes a common system. When one resists the power of this attraction, one, so far as it is possible, isolates himself from this common life. He shuts himself off into the outer darkness. There is no real solitude but that which one makes for one's self. Others may wrong and hate a man; but, if his heart be true to them, the community is still unbroken. When he shuts himself off by selfishness or hate, the separation is more real. The man that is full of his own schemings may not heed this at the moment, but the time may come when he will feel the awfulness of the solitude. In wrong-doing, one turns thus, not only against himself, but against that larger self in which is found his true being. It is himself against the universe of spiritual life. By such illustrations as these we may understand something of the weight of the obligation and the terror of the condemnation. We can understand why the obligation is not felt when one follows gladly the attraction of his nature, and why one recognizes its power so soon as one hesitates to obey it.

What is true of sympathy is true also of honor, in the ethical sense of that word. One who in private refuses to be bound by the principles which he is joining to enforce upon others sets himself apart from them in a little world of his own, if that can be called a world in which he stands alone. He who deceives sets up a barrier between himself and those about him. He who fails in his agreement has cut one of the bonds which binds him to his kind. He who yields to his lower passions degrades not only his own life, but that common life of which his is the manifestation.

The vague unconscious, or undefined, sense of this larger life is thus, as I conceive, the source of the sense of obligation and of repentance and of remorse. It first manifests itself in the impulses to kind and honorable acts, and later, as it has gathered strength, adds to these impulses its own authority.

I have thus considered simply the ultimate facts of ethics. Many influences coöperate with these. There is the force of education, of tradition, of law. Above all, there is the force of religion. My purpose has made it necessary to consider the facts of morality apart from this. The relation in which morality stands to religion, and the power which religion adds to it, form a theme too vast to be more than named in this connection. I will refer only to the sanction which even the lower forms of religion come in time to lend to the laws of righteousness, until, at last, when religion and morality have become absolutely interfused, the nature of both is transformed, and the moral law appears in the recognized majesty of Divinity.

THE NEW ETHICS.

We have seen that the fundamental principles of ethics remain the same, while the application of them may vary indefinitely. This variation results in part from a change of circumstances, and yet more from a change in the method of interpreting circumstances. Thus the ethics of one age may be, both in form and in practical results, very different from that of another. At the present day, we hear often of the "new ethics." The words imply the belief that a transformation such as has been referred to is now being accomplished; that, in some sense or other, the morality of the present age is assuming a type different in some respects from any that has been recognized in the past. Next in importance, then, to the study of the absolute principles of morality, is that of the form which these principles are taking on in the generation in which we live.

Among the phrases that have sprung from our

modern thought and life, there is none that seems to most so strange and ominous as this which speaks of a new morality. Men are slowly accustoming themselves to novelty in other things. All things else — the forms of government, even the forms of religion — concern the superstructure ; morality is the foundation. Disturb anything else, and the building may still stand ; disturb this, and the whole falls in ruin. Beneath a building of wood or stone one may place screws and hold it safely poised, while the underpinning is adjusted or even changed. Science, the result of ages of experience, may insure the safety of the new foundation. But what power shall hold poised the great structure of society while its foundation is renewed, and what science can assure us of the stability of supports as yet untried ?

The wise counsel of the preacher Robertson has comforted many a bewildered soul. No matter, he said in effect, how one may doubt in regard to spiritual matters ; so long as one holds fast to moral principle, one is safe. But how if this last support fails ? If the right gives way beneath the feet of him who hoped that he was on the eternal rock, what help or hope remains ?

And to many the new morality seems like no morality.

This dread is heightened by the immoralities of the time. When one meets example after example of brutality, which its nearness, perhaps also its comparative rarity, makes appear almost unprecedented, and of financial untrustworthiness in men who had been most loved and honored, one is tempted to hold the new ethics responsible for it all. Indeed, without deciding the questions at issue between the new and the old, we may admit some reason for this fear of change. Even if the old were no better than the new, the period of transition might be one of license.

In the ages of the past, we find traces of a like dread. Prominent among the charges brought by Aristophanes against Socrates was that of teaching a new morality. The father in the play sends his son to Socrates that he may learn some power of sophistry by which he can outwit his creditors; but he is disgusted when the son learns from the same teacher an art which renders of no effect his own paternal authority, and which, by a reversal of the time-honored relation between parent and child, forces the old man to submit to be flogged by the young representative of the new ethics.

But this very example suggests another aspect of the case. Socrates taught, indeed, a new morality; his contemporaries were filled with dread and anger; but the fresh foundation which he laid has been that upon which modern society has found rest. And was not Jesus the teacher of a new morality? "Ye have heard that it hath been said by them of old time; but I say unto you," — such was the form of his teaching. It was a new morality, setting itself up proudly and confidently against the old.

The theme, then, is a grave one. It concerns a matter where every change is full of peril; yet such a change in great epochs of the past has given new stability to human society, — has enabled it to rest secure through revolutions in thought and life. No place is here for rash experiment; but at the same time there is no place for a prejudice that shall condemn absolutely and unheard.

The theme has other difficulties. The new morality is something as yet incomplete. It is as yet largely tentative. It presents itself under various forms and in various degrees. Theories of morality, designed to illustrate, to support, or to complete the new ethics, have multiplied themselves in these latter days to an almost incredible extent. At the first glance it seems difficult, if not impossible, to determine to what the name actually belongs. A more careful observation shows, however, that beneath all these theories, and common to them all, are certain well-defined principles. . These have their marked characteristics. They may be easily and sharply distinguished from the principles of what I must, for the sake of the antithesis, call the old ethics. It is these principles that I have now to present and to illustrate.

In entering upon this discussion, I wish it understood that it is not my object to present, under the name of " The new morality," my own ethical views. My object is, to present a study of one aspect of the thought and life of the age in which we live, — something which is far more important than the views of any individual. The terms by which I shall describe this may seem to some terms of praise, and to others of blame. They are intended as neither. My aim is to approach the theme with historical or even judicial impartiality. But though this simply historical statement is my primary object, I shall, before concluding, attempt to estimate the worth of the new morality, and to determine to what extent, if at all, it is destined to replace the old.

The first contrast between what we must call the old ethics and the new, and perhaps the most important of all, is that the old morality is absolute, while the new is relative. According to the old, the question as to why the right is right has no place. The right is right, simply because it is right. The new is not content with this simple statement. It will go behind this absolute claim. It will demand its credentials of this absolute lawgiver. It asks, not in the spirit of rebellion but in that of scientific inquiry, what it is that makes the right right. At this very beginning there opens a gulf between the two that seems impassable. The old morality feels that to give any reason for right-doing, beyond the fact that it is right, would be to degrade righteousness. If right-doing had any other ground of authority than the moral law, this ground must be found in something higher than the moral law ; but the recognition of anything more authoritative than the moral law, it feels would be treason to morality. On the other hand, the new morality judges that if the right can give no reason for itself, it is unreasonable. It is ready to obey its law just as soon as the claim can be justified, and not before.

The breach between the two is widened when the new morality begins to answer its own question, and to show why the right, or what it calls such, should be obeyed. The right is right, it affirms, because it is useful. Utilitarianism, under one form or another, is the one principle common to all theories which represent the new morality ; and utilitarianism is what the old morality holds most in abhorrence. The antithesis of which it is most fond is that between the right and the expedient ; and utilitarianism takes the expedient, — the expedient in the largest possible sense of the term, it is true, — and places it on the throne of the right.

I have said that utilitarianism *under one form or another* is a principle common to all theories in which the new morality has taken form. I suppose that utilitarianism, pure and simple, may be considered as practically among the things of the past. This theory, it is easy to see, divided itself into two possible forms. According to the one, right action was based upon the advantage resulting directly or indirectly to the actor; according to the other, upon the advantage resulting to the community. It is easy to see that, so far as consequences to one's self are concerned, the consideration of these gives to actions no moral character whatever; and that if personal advantage be the end in view, there is no guarantee that the individual should not take the matter into his own hands, and seek to gain the ends that seem to him the best by the ways that seem to him the surest and the most direct. On the other hand, if advantage to the community be the end sought, the matter is left where the theory found it; for the question still presses, Why should the individual, at the cost of his own personal advantage, seek the public good? Further, this theory, in common with all theories that would base moral action upon some open, easily comprehended principle, according to which the individual should consciously guide his life, loses sight of the most important and efficient element of the moral law; I refer to the element of mystery. The moral law has owed its power, in a great measure, to the fact that it holds its seat in the secret recesses of the nature, or upon some inaccessible height above nature, from whence its demands issue with an authority not to be resisted or gainsaid. We may illustrate this aspect of the moral law by the discipline of a ship. Measured by the results, every act of every sailor, so far as the management of the ship is concerned, has for its end the general good. The sailors expose themselves to the fierceness of cold and tempest; they peril and often sacrifice their lives for the common cause. A stranger regarding their movements from the outside would find the most perfect exemplification of the utilitarian theory. But utility, though the measure and standard, is not the direct cause of their activity. If it were, a sailor might sometimes hesitate long before trusting himself on the perilous yard in the night and the tempest; or, even if all were well-disposed, the ship might go to the bottom while the men were discussing different possible methods of management. The source of authority is the captain's will. In the ship, his will has a mysterious and unquestioned supremacy. There is to be no hesitation and no discussion. The sailor does what he does, often having no guess as to the reason why. Utility, according to Kant's dictum in the larger field of morals, is the measure but not the cause of the activity. This illustrates the element which lends its peculiar authority to the moral law. If the new morality would in any sense replace the old, it must assert, as its vital element, some such principle as this. Morality must be shown to have at least the authority of an instinct.

The new ethics cannot give up the principle of utilitarianism, which is its life; but the difficulties with the doctrine as at first announced were too real to remain unnoticed. The doctrine was retained, and the difficulties which I have described were removed by one of the most ingenious and profound suggestions that have marked the history of thought. We have considered the principle of utility merely in relation to the life of the individual. We have supposed this life to begin without predisposition, and to be guided by conscious choice. Such was the view of the earlier teachers of utilitarianism. But let us take into account the great principle of heredity; let the sense of utility, of the needs of society, of the demands which the whole makes upon each part, have gathered strength through innumerable generations; let all irregularities of time and place be eliminated from the result, because such irregularities will go for nothing in the great mass ; and let the combined, intensified, and purified result enter into the constitution of the individual; let it be born with him, and twined in with every fibre of the brain: and we have a result far more satisfactory than any which we have before reached. This is the result which is taken for granted by the new ethics. In the language of Spencer, "The experiences of utility, organized and consolidated through all past generations of the human race, have been producing corresponding modifications, which by continued transmission and accumulation have become in us certain faculties of moral intuition."

We have thus the elements of a mysterious authority, whose decisions are not to be questioned or explained, which acts from the depths of the nature, and which thus represents the "categorical imperative" which we seek.

This result would seem at first sight to bring the new morality into greater harmony with the old. In reality it widens the breach between the two. We have seen the old ethics to be absolute, and the new relative, in their conceptions of the right. The old morality is further absolute in its conception of the source of moral authority in the soul. It insists that the moral instinct was one of the original endowments of man; or else, that the moral law is the direct voice of God making itself heard by the soul, whether it be willing or unwilling to listen. Upon this directness or spontaneity it bases much of its reverence for morality. According to the new ethics, the moral law is the outgrowth of experience. It is not that the soul has impressed itself upon the world; the world has moulded the soul. The moral law comes not from within, outward; it begins on the outside. It has its source in the circumstances of human life, not in that life itself.

One or two further considerations will bring the two systems into a yet sharper antithesis. The new morality insists that usefulness is the measure of right. Another question forces itself upon us, if the answer just given is to have any meaning. "The right is the useful:" the phrase says nothing till we know what is meant by usefulness. What is the great end its ministry for which gives any act moral preëminence? This question has been too much overlooked by utilitarian moralists, and the answer when given

has been sometimes as ambiguous as the phrase
it would explain.   Useful for happiness has, perhaps, been the most common explanation; but
this leaves the whole matter still open.   All men
seek happiness.   Who can say that the happiness
of the saint is greater than that of the sensualist?
By what test at the command of the utilitarian
can we decide that the one form of happiness
is of a higher grade, or a finer texture, than the
other?   The old morality has no difficulty in fur-
nishing such a test; the new has found in this
discrimination its hardest task.

And yet there is but one answer to the question, "Useful for what?" which the new morality, if it be wholly consistent with itself, can
give.   This answer must be found in the philosophy which underlies the thought most peculiar to the age; I mean the philosophy which is .
identified with the theory of development by
natural selection.   To the question under consideration, this philosophy can give but one answer,
namely, Useful for existence.   Its fundamental
principle is, "The Struggle for Existence."   Its
favorite phrase is, "The Survival of the Fittest."
In this phrase the word "fittest" means simply
that which is the best fitted to its surroundings,

that to which existence is therefore the easiest. Everything is tested by its adaptation to this end. The existence aimed at is mere existence. It does not mean primarily even happiness. Happiness of a certain kind is favorable to existence. There is no such drain upon the vital force as misery. Unhappiness gives a friction to life which makes living difficult. For this reason happiness has worth for the philosophy we are considering, not as an end in itself, but as a means to the end; and this end is existence. Its motto would be, not "The greatest good of the greatest number," whatever meaning may be implied by the word "good;" but, "The most prolonged existence for the greatest number." Still less, if possible, would the term "existence" include any moral quality. Morality, by its very definition, being synonymous with utility, and utility having reference to the mere fact of existence, existence can derive no nobility from this. A full existence has no advantage over an empty one, except that the full, having more points of contact with the world than the empty, has an advantage in the great struggle for life.

We have thus a fresh, and if possible a more striking, antithesis between the old and the new morality. To the old, goodness was the great end of life. It is for this that men live. Existence is for the sake of right-doing. To the new morality, right-doing is for the sake of existence. To the old, there is an impassable gulf between the moral demand and its fulfilment. Man exists in order to fulfil the moral law; and because this law is infinite in its requirements, man shall exist forever. To the new, man exists because he and his ancestors have on the whole done that which is right. His existence upon the earth is the reward of virtue.

We have thus compared the new ethics and the old, so far as their theoretical bases are concerned; and we have found them at every point sharply opposed to one another. We have now to consider the two in their practical relations. If they are as diverse in their requirements as they are in their theories, there can be only war between them as long as they shall both endure. If, however, we should find that, while differing so widely on all points of theory, they yet unite, to any considerable extent, in urging the same duties, then they may be co-workers to the same end. So far as the new morality is concerned, there is a still deeper question to be answered.

Can it furnish a basis for any system of practical
duties whatever ; or are its demands as variable
as the circumstances which make up the outward
life of man? As taught by Mr. Darwin, it would
seem to be open at least to doubt in this regard ;
and it was her perception of this fundamental
deficiency that drew from Miss Cobbe her indignant protest against the "Ethics of Darwinism." In this matter, however, we need not accept as final the words of any teacher. Even the
founder of a theory cannot be trusted to inter-
pret with infallible correctness all its manifold
relations. Neither accepting nor condemning
the results of any exponent of Darwinism, let us
look directly at the theory itself. We have then
to ask what form of human character does the
principle of natural selection tend to produce?
The general answer is, of course, that natural
selection tends to produce the character most in
harmony with its environment. But what, it
must be asked again, is meant by the environment? This has two forms. The first is the
natural and physical facts of the world; the
other is the structure of the society into which
any individual is born. So far as moral character is concerned, this last is the more impor-

tant.   In this aspect, the law of the survival of
the fittest has no reference to any fixed and arbi-
trary standard.   It means simply that he who is
best fitted to succeed in any community will
have the advantage, and will tend to impress his
moral nature upon his descendants.   There are
in the physical world certain fundamental characteristics which are necessary to life everywhere, and certain malformations that would be
fatal anywhere.   The blood must be oxygenated,
the food must be received and assimilated.   In
other respects the form varies infinitely.   There
may be innumerable degrees of strength, of size,
and of conformation and relation of organs.   If
the creature is to live in the water, or on the
land, or in the air; if its food is to be of one
kind or another; its whole structure will adapt
itself to these circumstances.   This adaptation
will descend to the most minute elements of the
environment.   It will answer to them as the clay
answers to its mould.   The same law of natural
selection produced the whale, the minnow, and
the devil-fish; the serpent, the sloth, and the
hare; the lion and the lamb; the hawk and the
dove.   If the social environment of man varies
less than the physical environment of the animal,

it varies no less really. There are, of course, certain kinds and degrees of immorality that are everywhere fatal to success. A certain degree of honor, the proverb tells us, is necessary if one would preserve his social standing in a company of thieves. But beyond the avoidance of the most gross and open violations of the social compact, there is little that is everywhere and always excluded by the demands of the social environment. The man who was fitted to succeed in the early days of the Roman republic would have failed in the latter days of the empire; and one whom the social elements of the empire pushed into prominence would have fared hardly in the republic. Thus the social environment is ever changing, and the demands made upon the moral nature by success vary indefinitely. Indeed, the societies in which the highest and finest moral attributes are a passport to success are very rare. The "fittest" in the moral sense and the "fittest" in the sense of Darwinism are not often the same. Certainly, neither in Athens nor at Jerusalem was moral perfection one with fitness to survive; and Mr. Gregg has fairly proved to us that in European society the law of the survival of the fittest has, in many ways, opposed

the production and survival of the best. If the
new morality have no better basis than this law,
it rests upon very sandy foundations ; or, if we
regard the present relation of the social factors
as one of stable equilibrium, our moral code must
be, to a large extent, reconstructed ; and in this
reconstruction the demands of what has been
generally recognized as the moral nature must
be largely ignored.

Further, it is often insisted that natural selection means simply the right of the strongest ;
that an ethical theory based upon this would
simply affirm the right of the strongest in our
human fellowships. It is probably from some
such view of the ethics of Darwinism that a bril-
liant though anonymous writer refers thus to an
author who had affirmed his belief in Darwinism. "We do not believe," he says, "that this
author is at all prepared to accept the changes
which this new view of the laws of growth would
work in practical ethics, in our treatment of
paupers and criminals, for example, and our
views of marriage and culture, We doubt if he
is ready to say that it is vastly more important
to prevent a criminal from having descendants
than it is to reform him ; and we are confident

that he does not regard it as being as much the duty of healthy men to marry young as to acquire culture and do great deeds; more wrong to marry a sickly person for love than a strong one for money. And these new ethics will find as little to support them in the ascetic self-subjugation of the older time as in the sentimental fear of taking life of the new."

I do not know whether the writer from whom I have just quoted is or is not in sympathy with Darwinism, and with the system of ethics that he believes to grow out of it; whether the passage was written in good faith or as satire. In this view, "the struggle for existence" is one in which physical strength and worldly wisdom are the great weapons of success. Even from this point of view it would be difficult to make the statement quite consistent with itself, — to explain, for instance, why a criminal should be killed in order that he might have no descendants; and the person who sees in marriage only a form of money-making should be encouraged to have them; why it is so much worse to violate the laws of property than to degrade the highest moral instincts; why worse to obtain money on a fraudulent promise of repayment of money, than to obtain, we will say, money under a fraudulent promise of repayment in love.

To see the full bearing of the passage, we need to look behind one or two phrases. To marry for money is not necessarily to marry according to the laws of health ; to marry for love is not necessarily to marry unhealthily. In a community where self-interest should control all marriages, not all the descendants would be healthy ; but all would, in time, be selfish. In a community where all marriages should be for love, all the descendants would not be unhealthy, but there would be a tendency to unselfishness in all.

It is not my business, however, to explain, to justify, or to condemn, the passage I have quoted. I have referred to it simply to illustrate what I conceive to be a very common view of the kind of morality which would result if Darwinism should become the established philosophy of the time. Perhaps also it illustrates the change and confusion in regard to the standard of morality which would actually be produced by recognition, in its fullest extent, of the law of natural selection as we have thus far regarded it.

But there is another aspect of this law. It

has a broader field of application than any which we have thus far considered, and in this broader field its demands are absolute and inflexible.

I may introduce a consideration of this new aspect of the case by reference to a difficulty which Mr. Darwin tells us he met while working out his system. The difficulty was suggested by the presence of the sterile workers among the bees. This seemed at first sight, he tells us, fatal to his whole theory. It is obvious that sterility is nothing that can be hereditary. Moreover, even the tendency to sterility is di-. rectly opposed to the success of any class of beings in the struggle for existence. Soon, however, the thought of the great naturalist took a wider range. Any class of individuals, considered merely as individuals, with whom such a tendency should exist, would tend to extinction : but a community is not merely a collection of individuals ; it is itself an individual. The principle of natural selection applies as really to communities as to the individuals that compose them. These also are subjected to the struggle for existence, and here also it is the fittest who survive. The community of bees that should develop a class of sterile workers would have thereby an immense advantage over those that did not, and would endure while they would perish. Schopenhauer had long before expressed the thought that the community of bees, for example, develops classes of members adapted to special functions, just as a body develops organs. And now Darwin shows that these organizations are as plastic under the great force which controls the development of life as the single organisms themselves. Thus the difficulty that threatened the destruction of the Darwinian theory was a means of opening to it a wide sweep of applications, of which its founder at first had not dreamed.

The same principle comes to our aid in seeking in the theory of Darwinism a basis for morality. We have found that the principle of natural selection would vary in its action according to the nature of the social environment. One society would favor the development of honesty and honor; another that of cunning and hypocrisy. In one, gluttony and sensuality and kindred vices would sink a man to the lowest stratum of society; in another they would buoy him up so that he should float upon the highest. But here at last we have a principle to which

these social conditions are themselves amena-
ble. One society will develop one type of character; another, another; but according to the
type of character which it favors will it stand
or fall. Here we find a recognition by the facts
of history of the fundamental distinctions of
right and wrong. What we call righteousness is
the only enduring basis upon which society can
rest. We are told much of the "Power not ourselves that makes for righteousness." We have,
perhaps, all wished that the author of the phrase
would explain to us more clearly the method of
the working of this power. Here at last it manifests itself. It is present as a power of judgment, if not of creation. The nations that work
iniquity, that despise justice, that lose themselves
in the revels of the senses, are at last dashed
to pieces like a potter's vessel; and a purer,
stronger, and less corrupted race succeeds.

We see, thus, how the principle of natural selection may, and often does, fall into collision
with itself. Under one form it develops a type
of character which under another it destroys.
In the Roman empire it was this that led the
Caracallas and the Caligulas to the supreme
position; and it was this that destroyed the Ro-

man empire, because its social conditions were such as to foster the growth of characters like those to whom I have referred. Such is the irony of this ruler of the world..

The general conditions of human society are the same everywhere. In a valuable article upon the "Ethics of Darwinism,"[1] Mr. Francis E. Abbot has compared these conditions to the fundamental relations which make mathematics an *a priori* science. These are the principles in accordance with which the terrible power of natural selection works in the large relations which we are here considering.

Perhaps, indeed, it is to this larger aspect of the case that the passage which I quoted a short time ago refers. I mean the passage in which physical strength was made the one supreme thing, in which a calculating meanness that favored this was exalted so high above a generous love that ignored it, in which the natural sympathies of the heart were to be suppressed in order that vice and poverty might be suppressed in their turn. Here at last may be the field where the survival of the fittest means simply the survival of the strongest; where the struggle for

[1] *Index*, March 12, 1874.

existence leaves no place for delicacy, or refinement, or idealism, or chivalric extravagance;
where all must be calculating and hard, and a
sensible selfishness is more to the purpose than
an extravagant love. But even in this battle of
the Titans, this struggle for existence, in which
it is nation against nation and race against race,
such teaching misinterprets the laws that pre-
side over the great strife.

These laws are gentle as they are terrible.
See their working in the life-and-death conflict
which is waged in the whole realm of the lower
nature, in which bird and beast secure their
place in this over-crowded world, where each survives only at the cost of multitudes that perish.
Here, if anywhere, would be manifested the
sternness of these laws, their contempt for anything but brute force. Shall we utter here
teaching such as that to which I have referred?
Shall we say, Strength is everything; in this
fierce battle he who can best seize his prey and
fight down his rivals in the chase will be the victor? Shall we bid the nightingale seek weapons
like those of the hawk, and the humming-bird
change its iridescent garment for an armor of
hard shell that shall protect its tiny life? Little

shall we understand the powers that determine the result of the strife, and award his triumph to the victor. To them the delicate, the graceful, the tender, the beautiful, are as dear as the fierce and the strong. It was the great law of natural selection itself that taught the nightingale to sing, and that painted the humming-bird with his changeful hues. It is this that whispers to the timid hare to flee, and this that binds the gentle sheep together in their harmless federation.

Those who maintain that, according to the law of natural selection, only the strong survive, seem to forget for the moment how the helpless young of species the most unlike, the fiercest as well as the gentlest, are cared for by self-forgetful and often self-sacrificing love.

What is true in the lower world of animal life is no less true in the higher world of man. Here the struggle is no less terrible. Here, also, in the long run, it is the fittest that survives. Long before Darwinism was dreamed of, Emerson sang in his prophetic numbers, —

> " For gods delight in gods,
> And thrust the weak aside."

But there is another kind of might than hard, gross, bodily force, and in the struggle for exist-

ence the battle is not always to the physically
strong. Two elements have contributed more
than anything else to the success of man in the
conflict with the lower animals, and of the civilized man in conflict with the barbarian. One
of these is knowledge, or the power of thought;
the other is the force of the social instincts.
Ideas on the one hand, a self-forgetful devotion
on the other, — these are what have won for the
higher races the victory. Whatever checks the
tendency either to mental development on the
one side, or spiritual development on the other,
strikes the heaviest possible blow at the stability
of the social organism.

Physical strength, brute force, whether of body
or will, is nothing to be spoken lightly of. It is
something to be sought and cherished by wise
prevision. It is only when the lower force is
urged in despite of the higher spiritual forces
that we protest. Sleek and prosperous selfishness gives a certain element of strength to a society. For a time it may furnish to it a stable
foundation. But it furnishes a power of disin-
tegration as well. In times of peril, selfishness
will give its money, it will not give its life, for
the common cause. It is not the children of a

line of ancestors who have been bound together in each generation by the golden bands of self-interest that, in a moment of peril, a nation can summon to its defence. It is not those who have learned to repress the natural instincts of humanity, who see no longer the sacredness of human life, who are willing to extirpate suffering by the extirpation of the sufferers, — it is not these that can catch the grand enthusiasm which makes men willing to die before they know whether the good they seek can actually be purchased even at that costly price. I am not comparing these different types of character by any sentimental standard. I am bringing them before the bar of that stern power which is now recognized as the judge of all the earth ; and it is in the light of its judgments that I affirm that he who urges on the authority of Darwinism the hard morality that has been described, has failed to comprehend the working of those laws of which he speaks.

There is no tenderness of human love, there is no generosity of human charity, there is no self-forgetfulness of a sublime idealism, that does not have its place and its work, even under the hard and stern conditions of the struggle for existence.

A community may be constructed on principles that will crush out these self-forgetting lives. The laws of natural selection applied in the narrow circuit of this community may justify and enforce their extinction. But there is a higher court which sits also for the enforcing of these laws. To this higher court the appeal is always made. At this tribunal the lower decision is reversed; and the community which has disowned all that is tender, and chivalric, and self-forgetful will in its turn suffer terrible condemnation.

Our twofold question is thus answered. The law of natural selection furnishes a basis for an absolute morality, above all fluctuations resulting from conditions peculiar to special times and places; and this morality is, on the whole, one with that which the best thought of the world has recognized as such. I do not raise the question whether the existence of the moral sense may or may not be explained by this principle. We have found simply that there is no need for fear lest the new science shall undermine virtue. We have found a force working steadily in the direction of a high morality, and have reached a point where the new ethics and the old are in accord.

The two systems, then, while theoretically at absolute variance, are practically working together towards the same end. This fact may suggest the question whether the theoretical antagonism between the two implies a real hostility; whether the antithesis may not rather be called polar; whether they do not represent opposite sides of the same thing, or are not the outgrowths of opposite but inseparable tendencies of thought and life. An examination will show that this is the case. There are recognized in the thought of most, and in the practical life of all, two principles, in appearance utterly antagonistic to one another. These are the principles of freedom and necessity. Logically destructive of one another, practically they are recognized as common factors of life.

Theodore Parker once gave, if I remember rightly, about three parts out of a hundred of the result of any life to freedom, the rest to necessity. Really, the relation is a variable one; in some lives, even the "three parts" would be hard to find. In others, freedom is a constantly increasing factor. These principles have embodied themselves in the systems of morality we have been considering. The old morality represents

the idea of freedom ; the new, that of necessity.
According to the old, every man is the absolute
master of himself ; according to the .new, every
man is the creature of circumstances. I have
said that in common life both these principles
are practically recognized. The parent believes
that the character of his child is ultimately to
rest upon the choice of the child himself; yet he
seeks by education and surroundings to force the
child into the ways of virtue, and to ward off evil
influences, as if the child were wholly at their
mercy. I am not going to discuss the old question, and to seek a solution of the difficulties that
so many have found insoluble. It is enough for
us here to have found the secret of the divergence between the two systems of ethics, and to
recognize the fact that, till the old strife between
freedom and necessity is at an end, each of these
systems will find its place and its work.

Another consideration may help us to understand how two systems, practically in accord,
may stand theoretically in such sharp antithesis, even while it contributes nothing toward
the solution of this antithesis. I refer to the
partialness of each statement. It is easy to see
that both end in incompleteness. The one

affirms an absolute right which can neither be explained nor justified; the other makes its highest term existence, without object or fulfilment. But the law of right implies imperfection in its subject, for the moral law, as such, exists so far as love is absent. As the Jewish law was the schoolmaster to lead men to Christ, so the moral law everywhere prepares the way for, or takes the place of, a wise and thoughtful love. As Jesus said, "Love is the fulfilling of the law."

On the other hand, the law of natural selection itself may show us how the individual exists in and for the community. This is only a statement from the outside of that which, when consciously adopted as the true meaning of life, is expressed from the inside as the law of love. The maker of the musical instrument aims simply to produce accuracy and purity of tone. Who could tell in advance the magnificence of the result when the single instrument lends itself to form part of the grand harmony of the completed composition? The law of natural selection aims at existence only; but when the existence of the individual is given up for that of the whole, there come a beauty and glory that transfigure the result.

In spite of the fundamental accord between the two systems in practical relations, the different principles which they embody will introduce superficial yet very marked differences into the practical working of the two types of morality.

I. The old morality is stern. It judges pitilessly, throwing the burden of his misdeeds wholly upon the wrong-doer. The new is gracious and sympathetic. It seeks excuses and palliations; so far as it blames at all, and its blame is simply the seeking of the nearest cause of the result, it lays the burden of the guilt, not on the wrong-doer himself, but upon the society that has made him what he is.

II. The old morality is unpractical. It utters its commands, and leaves them to execute themselves. The new is practical. It seeks so to arrange the circumstances of each life that its demands shall inevitably be fulfilled.

III. The old morality, though terribly radical when its way is perfectly clear before it, is yet often blindly conservative. Having confessedly no outward test of right and wrong, it sometimes confounds traditions and prejudices with intuitions. It adopts some institution as divinely given, or as expressing some fundamental element of right, and launches the terrors of its wrath against all who would disturb it. The new has an external test; namely, utility. This test it applies fearlessly. It is thus absolutely radical. For it the prestige of years, the claims of divine appointment or of inherent sanctity, amount to nothing. The whole world is open to its reforming touch.

In this comparison the old morality may appear at some disadvantage; but we must bear in mind that if the new morality could entirely supplant it, there would remain no morality worthy of the name. It is the free act of the soul in choosing the right that gives to it any moral character in the highest sense of the word. We may make this choice easy and natural, or we may surround it with difficulties; but in any case it is this which is, morally speaking, the vital point of every act.

IV. The old morality placed itself outside of all historical relations. The moral sense being one of the original constituents of human nature, it existed from the first fully formed. The only historical change which it can undergo is that of a greater or less debasement. The new morality recognizes the principle of development in moral relations as well as in all others. Nowhere has greater intellectual activity been displayed than in the search for the conditions under which the germs of the moral sense first present themselves, and those under which it arises to an ever fuller consciousness of its own nature. These circumstances cannot, I believe, account for the existence of the moral idea, any more than, in the wise judgment of its founder, the theory of natural selection can account for life. But the moral principle, like life, must have had a beginning in the world and a history. There must have been conditions under which alone its first and lowest manifestations were possible, and those which have controlled the form of its development. Let it be that it is in its source supernatural; it must yet, as the Christian Church itself could teach us in the story of its founder, be born out from and into the conditions of the earthly history. Thus, though we need to receive with the most cautious criticism all historical results offered to account for the rise of morality in the world, though there needs to be placed a check on the rashness of speculation that thinks it has accounted for everything the history of which it has described, we may have only welcome for all efforts to throw light upon the genesis of the moral idea, and thus to solve questions perhaps the most important and the most difficult of any that grow out of our human history.

Let us now glance at certain of the practical methods of the new ethics, in order to find illustrations of some of the characteristics that have been described.

It need hardly be remarked that in the new morality it is the active virtues that bear the palm. It was once enough, as Thoreau phrases the contrast, that the saint was good; he must now show himself to be good for something. Virtue is not merely a system of moral gymnastics; it is the striving towards certain definite practical results. In this effort the most delicate social problems receive a fresh solution, and the most fundamental relations a fresh adjustment.

The institution of marriage offers itself as one of the most striking examples of such treatment. This will be clear if we consider the present general recognition of divorce, and that the only churches which absolutely condemn divorce, and forbid their clergy to marry parties that have been divorced, are those which are bound most firmly to the old order.

The relation of husband and wife, and in general the relation of woman to the state, has undergone a like change. The new morality recognizes no superiority or inferiority between the sexes. It may admit that husband and wife are one, but it watches with impartial interest to see, as the old phrase has it, which is the one. Or rather it regards them as two, each having special interests, that may stretch immeasurably on either side beyond what is included in the little life of the family. Of the tendencies that would press beyond the limits I have named, that would do away with the restraints of marriage or with marriage itself, I do not speak. These represent not the new morality, but the old immorality.

In the larger realm of the state, we find like changes. Indeed, here the relation of things has been completely inverted. Men used to speak of the divine right of the king; now the talk is of the divine right of the people. Before, the great stress was laid upon submission to the powers that be; now the great stress is laid upon the duty of governments to their citizens. A man's duties to the state are those which he wears the lightest.

The relation of the different members of the state to one another has been also changed. Especially is this true of the relation between the rich and the poor. The time has been when poverty was felt to be, to some extent, a mark of sanctity. Your tramp would lack little of being regarded, if not as a saint, at least as a very good representative of one. Poverty was regarded as, in a double sense, a means of grace. The poor themselves were not far from the kingdom of heaven; at the same time they furnished one of the readiest means of salvation to their richer neighbors. It was the poor who carried the souls of the rich to heaven. Thus poverty was to be comforted and solaced. It was to be in some superficial way ameliorated. The poor were at any event to be kept alive. But the idea of doing away with poverty would have been considered, if not sacrilegious, at least hardly desirable. The life of poverty was indeed the ideal life. This whole state of things has changed. "God's poor," said the old morality; "the Devil's poor," would say the new if it spoke its whole thought. Poverty is not the blessing, but the curse, of society. The whole social effort is not so much to ameliorate it as to abolish it.

Charity, instead of being regarded as the ideal virtue, is, at least under its old form, regarded as a weakness if not as a vice. "If you would help men," cries the new morality, "help them to help themselves." "Give to him that asketh thee," cried the old. "Give to nobody that asks thee," cries the new; "send beggars to the central committee;" and to this central committee it says, "If you give anything, give work." In harmony with its fundamental principle, the new morality, in its most exaggerated form, would like to withhold aid altogether, to leave only the fittest to survive. Since, happily, it cannot so far suppress the natural feelings of its followers, it would at least simply help men to be able to hold their own in the great struggle. Believing in the controlling influence of the environment, it would seek to bring into the surroundings of the poor all cheerful and healthful influences. When superfluities are to be given to the sick or the needy, the old morality would give, perhaps, tracts; the new gives flowers and fruits. Its great instrument is, under one form or another, education. Its highest ambition is, however, to so use the laws of *heredity* as to reach the best results. It would introduce, if it knew how, the principle of artificial selection. It is, however, still wrestling with the lower problem, and has hardly dared to face the higher. We have as yet working towards that end little save statistics, — those advance-couriers of reform. The new morality in its natural unexaggerated shape is not less charitable than the old ; it is even more so. It is more difficult to study all the circumstances of the life of a poor person, and then to help him as he may need, than it is to make a careless gift of money ; just as the practice of a scientific physician is more toilsome than that of a quack who has his one panacea for every ill. And when, in the future, men look back upon the path up which the race has climbed, I believe that the saints of what we call the new morality will receive a homage of gratitude and praise equal, at least, to that rendered to the noblest saints of the old.

The treatment of vice by the new morality is akin to its treatment of poverty. Heredity, education, and social surroundings are the influences which it would use for its suppression. The old morality would teach the evils of intemperance. The new would ·open the " People's Club " and the " Holly Tree Inn." Its methods may be in-

sufficient ; we may be discouraged by seeing the
moral failure of those born and nurtured apparently under the most ideal circumstances ; but
still its methods are those which are indispensable for the best results. They are indispensable,
but they are not sufficient. As the free choice,
on which the old morality insists, is, as we have
seen, the one vital point in any act by which it
has moral quality, so the appeal to this, under
one form or another, the arousing in a man the
sense of being the master of himself and of his
own destinies ; the sense of the absoluteness,
even of the awfulness, of the right, — all of this
must form a part, and the highest part, of any
system of moral training, if it is to be what its
name implies.

In this discussion I have used the words "new"
and "old" in a somewhat loose and general sense.
I have not certainly meant to imply that all the
characteristics which I have described as those
of the new ethics are peculiar to the morality of
this generation. Already, in the beginning of
Christianity, we find some of the most important
of them expressed. The saying of Jesus, " The
Sabbath is made for man, not man for the Sabbath," is as thoroughly utilitarian as any saying

could be. It illustrates even the utilitarian radicalism. A like radicalism we find yet more strongly embodied in the teaching of Paul, who sought to emancipate his brethren from the whole ceremonial law of the Jews, not even deterred by the thunders of Sinai and the sacredness of the tables of Moses, from including the Sabbath itself among the forms that were to become obsolete. The prayer of Jesus, " Father, forgive them, for they know not what they do," and the cry of the apostle, "Consider thyself, lest thou also be tempted," embody the same kind of gracious considerateness that we found to characterize the new morality. What is lacking is the practicality that comes from the development of the science of political economy, and the historical results which had no place in the scheme of the early Church, even had they been within the reach of its founders. At the same time the New Testament ethics are all alive with that consciousness of human responsibility which forms the chief characteristic of what I have called the old morality. We see thus strikingly illustrated the possibility of a practical reconciliation of the two types. We see also an element which the new morality must never leave out of the account, if it would perform its work aright.

We have already referred to the higher principle of love, towards which both forms of ethics point as the fulfilling of all law. The fact that primitive Christianity was the embodied love may help us to understand how it could hold in solution elements so diverse. We see also the greatest need of the new morality, and perhaps its greatest peril. Dealing as it so largely does with statistics, starting as it does with great general principles, it may be in danger of looking upon men too much in the mass. The truest helpfulness does not recognize what are called the masses; or, if it recognizes them, it is only that it may disintegrate the mass. It has to do with individuals. It loves not merely man; still more does it love men. It was this warmth and tenderness of personal relationship that lent sometimes a certain charm even to what were otherwise the most repulsive forms of the old *régime;* and it is this that the new morality must know how to blend with its love of principles, if it would replace, or more truly if it would worthily fulfil, the Christian ideal.

IV. CONCLUSION.

POETRY, COMEDY, AND DUTY,

CONSIDERED IN THEIR RELATION TO ONE ANOTHER.

WE have thus far considered poetry, comedy, and duty in their separateness. We have now to indicate, very briefly, their relation to one another. However little they may seem to have in common, they together fill out one of the most important departments of the mental life.

It is evident that the word "poetry" must here be used in its largest and freest sense. "Comedy" and "duty" are generic terms. "Poetry," in the strict sense of the word, and in the sense in which I have thus far used it, is specific. It represents one form of art, while art itself, represents one form of beauty. Poetry may, however, stand as the representative of the whole æsthetic side of life; and, indeed, this freer use is not wholly foreign to the common employment of the term.

Poetry, comedy, and duty represent each a special relation to the environment, so far as this is regarded independently of any personal end. Science, philosophy, and religion, indeed, stand very close to the field thus indicated. Science and philosophy are, however, originally seekers. So far as fixed results are reached, these are passed over to the practical and the ideal life, and divided between them: that is, either they are adopted into the world of personal ends; or else they are made objects of æsthetic delight, as we rejoice in the beauty and sublime order of the cosmos that is revealed to us; or they give new breadth and sublimity to the law of duty. Religion, on the other hand, represents a relation to an environment regarded as known. In it, however, personal relations have a place; and in it the sense of beauty and the moral sense find their fullest development. The department that we have assigned to poetry, comedy, and duty thus belongs to them alone. They together make up our relation to the environment ideally considered; this environment being made known to us by the ordinary experience of life, and in a truer way by science, philosophy, and religious faith.

The perception of the comic and the enjoyment of beauty are both purely contemplative. They represent, however, different forms of contemplation, and wholly different attitudes towards its object.

In the enjoyment of beauty, the relation is one of absolute sympathy. The spirit feels itself so at one with nature that the freedom and strength of nature give it joy through the very beholding of them. In the comic there is a complete absence of sympathy. The spirit holds itself wholly apart from and above the object of its contemplation. So far as the world and life are considered as comic, the spirit stands over against them as truly as if it belonged to another sphere. Not only does it survey the objects of its laughter without sympathy; as we have seen, it groups them according to its own mood and caprice, and not according to their own fundamental and essential relations. In the comic we have thus the meeting of two most widely sundered moods of the soul. In one aspect it appears to be the most trivial element of life; yet in it we find the most complete self-assertion of the spirit. This self-assertion consists in the fact that the spirit has given up

all sense of bondage to the world, of responsibility towards it, and even of sympathy with it.
It desires nothing and it regrets nothing. It
neither loves nor hates. It is simply amused.
It stands complete in itself, and content with
this completeness.

We may here see the significance of the fact
referred to in our previous discussion, that the
perception of the comic is peculiar to man. We
find the beginnings of the sense of beauty, even
of the moral sense, among the animals. It is
doubtful if there is with them any hint of the
sense of the ludicrous. It is odd that this lightest aspect of life is the one in which the independence of the spirit most manifests itself. In
this connection, it is interesting to notice that
Homer recognized laughter as one of the marks
of divinity. The "inextinguishable laughter"
of the gods marked their exaltation above all
the entanglements and perplexities of life. It
separated them more truly from the world than
their undisturbed bliss did the gods of Epicu-
rus. It does not matter that, according to the
Homeric story, the laughter of the gods was
not inextinguishable ; that the sufferings and
the contests of men brought trouble and dissen-

sion to the celestial minds; that jealousies and rancors found a place there. The phrase shows an ideal of the divine life, even if the ideal was not ·realized.

Because in the comic is found a special characteristic of the spirit, and its act of purest or most independent self-assertion, it does not follow that the recognition of the ludicrous is the highest mood of the soul, or that "inextinguishable laughter" is the truest type of life. That which is most characteristic need not be that which is most habitual. Because one has "a giant's strength" it does not follow that one need always "use it like a giant." The spirit, in spite of the possibility of thus severing itself from any sense of bondage to the world, is not a thing apart that can find its truest existence in this isolation. It is a fundamental principle of the spiritual life, that the truest function of independence is that of self-surrender.

> "Our wills are ours, we know not how;
> Our wills are ours, to make them Thine."

In the enjoyment of beauty the spirit is no longer in solitude. It rejoices in the life about it, in that life of which it feels itself a part. The relation is still, however, of the nature of play. The difference is that while in the comic the spirit makes sport of the world, in the enjoyment of beauty it shares the play of the common life. There is a sense of freedom and exaltation. The spirit stands on equal terms with the world about it, except as the superiority of the world is shown by its lavishness. The spirit is the recipient of the best gift of the outward nature; that is, the gift of herself. It is a recipient only and need make no return.

In duty the relation has become yet more profound. The spirit feels the power of the laws that control the universe. Earnestness has taken the place of play. Subjection has taken that of freedom. It is a subjection, indeed, by which the spirit feels itself ennobled. There is a dignity in duty that is absent from the play of the comic; a grandeur that is absent even from the joy of beauty.

In the comic, then, we have an indication of that independence of the spiritual life by which it is fitted for the highest destiny. In the enjoyment of beauty, and in obedience to the law of righteousness, this destiny is fulfilled. In the comic, the freedom of the spirit is an empty freedom. In the enjoyment of beauty the spirit, while no less free than before, finds its joy in the concrete reality of the world. In duty it has found an object worthy of its highest devotion, and has surrendered itself to this, finding in this surrender the full and free realization of itself.

We have thus far, in the comparison, regarded poetry as representing in general the poetic or æsthetic side of life. If we take the term in its narrower and more literal sense, we find that poetry and duty are both creators. Both seek to embody an ideal in some perfectly fitting shape. Poetry produces its creations to supplement the world. Art rears temples, which, in the words of Emerson already quoted, nature adopts into her race. Shakespeare creates a world of characters and events which takes its place by the side of the world of actual persons and events. Duty, on the other hand, seeks to embody its ideal in life. It seeks not to supplement, but to transform, the actual. The relation of comedy to these two, so far as this aspect of the case is concerned, is primarily that of pure and direct negation. Not merely does comedy recognize no ideals; in its freest and largest sweep it denies them, and makes war upon the very semblance of them. From this point of view, the Mephistopheles of Goethe is the incarnation of laughter.

The comic depends, however, as we have already seen, upon the character, mood, or standpoint of the individual. We must not forget that there are two positions which are diametrically opposed to one another : that of Mephistopheles, and that of the earnest spirit which is striving to fulfil the highest ideals of life. Each is ridiculous to the other. The very essence of Mephistopheles is that to him all ideals are intrinsically and absolutely absurd. From the other point of view, Mephistopheles is seen to be more ridiculous than the world appeared to him. To live among the infinite realities, to live within the reach of the inspiration that comes from the beauties and sublimities of nature and from the heroic deeds of man, and to find only emptiness and vanity, — this, as seen from the higher vantage-ground, is the height of absurdity. Thus the great heroes of the world have often been also good laughers.

When we studied the comic as such, we saw that there was nothing laughable in itself. When we look at the matter in relation to poetry and duty, we see that there is another side to this truth. The sense of the comic is not the only or the supreme factor in human nature. The sense of beauty and the moral sense have also their place in the normally developed mind. What appears absurd to the fully developed spirit may, in a sense, be regarded as absurd in itself. The difference between that which is ludicrous to it and that which is ludicrous to the mere mocker is still merely subjective; but it is the difference between the subjectivity of a nature which is rounded and complete, and that of one which lacks some of the most important elements of the spiritual life. The aspect of the universe varies, indeed, with our point of view; but we must believe that there is a true point of view which we can approximate, although we may never reach it. Even from this the comic is not excluded, and the mind is imperfect that has no recognition of it. Not only may the spirit be refreshed by the comicalities that are merely superficial; the lower life, as we have seen, has its absurd as well as its tragic aspect. Thus comedy may be the helper of the higher life in which the love of beauty and the moral sense have the controlling place.

Comedy is the corrector as truly as the helper of the earnest life. Without it the poetic may become the sentimental, and the heroic the burlesque.

Thus we cannot enough admire the completeness of the relation between these three. Comedy, within its due place, keeps the spirit sane. Through it the spirit preserves the freshness and bloom of its life, even while it surrenders itself to the charms of beauty, and yields itself to be the instrument of "the Power that makes for righteousness." The path of duty is, indeed, the path of life; but happy is he who can press, sometimes laughing and sometimes singing, upon his way.